The Chocolate Egg Sanford 3rd Age Cl[ub]

David W Robinson

in association with Ocelot Press

This edition © 2024 David W Robinson

Edited by Maureen Vincent-Northam

No part of this book may be used or reproduced in any manner whatsoever without written permission of the author except for brief quotations used for promotion or in reviews. This is a work of fiction. Names, characters, and incidents are used fictitiously.

First published by Darkstroke Books 2013

Chapter One

A gust of wind hit the bus broadside as it turned and crossed a bridge over the main railway line into Weston-super-Mare. From the jump seat, looking down on the railway station, Joe Murray could see a small army of people making their way out of the station, presumably having just arrived by train.

Another gust of wind hit the bus, lashing rain onto the windows, and Joe felt the vehicle shudder. 'Great weekend this is gonna turn out,' he grumbled.

Sat behind him, Brenda Jump cast a wistful glance through the windows. 'Shame too. I thought it might have been sunny. I like sunshine at Easter.'

'When I was married, me and Alison used to go to Blackpool for the day every Easter,' Joe said. 'Yes, and it never stopped raining there, either.'

Alongside Brenda, Sheila Riley leaned forward and gave him a friendly shove on the shoulder. 'Don't be so mean, Joe. I'm sure you and Alison had some wonderful moments.'

'We did,' he agreed. 'Especially when she was at the bingo and I was in the pub.'

Turning his back on them and their disparaging responses, he, too, gazed at the rain blowing in sheets across the approaching seafront of Weston-super-Mare.

It had rained consistently throughout the two

hundred-mile journey from Sanford, but not as heavily as it was coming down now. It seemed as if the weather gods had reserved their worst efforts for their arrival.

Joe glanced at the large dial of his Rotary watch and read just after 2.00pm. Six hours since they left Sanford, and they had stopped only once, on a service station outside Alvechurch when Keith, their long-suffering driver, needed to take a legal break from driving.

'Normally, I'd do it in four and a half hours,' he had told Joe while they crawled through a large jam east of Birmingham, 'but it's Good Friday tomorrow, so every dipstick and his wife is on the road today, and the weather just makes it worse.'

There were further delays due to an accident on the outskirts of Gloucester and again near Bristol, where the M5 met the M4, and the two Severn crossings added to the crowded roads.

'I'll be glad when I'm like you lot; an old git,' Keith had grumbled. 'Then I can sit back and let someone else do the driving.'

When he eventually accelerated away from the jam and across the Avonmouth Bridge, he asked, 'What possessed you to come all this way? Normally you don't go further than a hundred miles for your weekend jaunts.'

Joe had shrugged. 'The members decide, not me. Personally, I'm with you. I'd rather go to Scarborough, or at a pinch, Cleethorpes. I don't like spending most of the first day travelling, and at least you can get to the Yorkshire coast in an hour.'

As Keith came off the motorway and turned towards Weston, Joe had rolled a cigarette, ready for their arrival, and commented, 'It could be worse. Sheila and Brenda keep going on about a week in Tenerife.'

'Well I'm not driving you there. Not a bad idea, though.'

'Crap idea for me. My ex-wife lives there.'

Joe sank into his thoughts until Keith had to brake sharply, bringing Joe back to reality.

A middle-aged woman, her hair a shock of red, had crossed in front of the bus. She carried a large handbag over one arm, and clutched a large, boxed Easter egg under the other. Judging from the direction in which she was walking, Joe assumed she had come from the railway station, but while most of the pedestrians had paused to look both ways, she had not.

Driving slowly on, Keith opened his window. 'You wanna learn to look what's coming before you cross the road, luv, or your grandkids won't get to eat the chocolate egg.' Joe did not hear her response, but when Keith said, 'and the same to you', he guessed it was not complimentary.

Muttering to himself, with occasional glances at his satnav display, Keith negotiated a large roundabout, and steered the bus towards the town centre. Passing familiar High Street names, most of them busy with people eager to be out of the rain, Joe had his first glimpse of the seafront half a mile ahead, and when Keith finally turned right along the promenade, in the direction of the Grand Pier, Joe sensed a wave of relief run through the seventy members on the bus. He reasoned that in common with Keith, if the members had realised what a toil the journey would be, they would probably have voted for Scarborough.

'Two minutes, Joe,' Keith warned him.

Joe reached up and behind to collect the PA microphone, switched it on and tapped the head to ensure it was working. Standing to face his members, he announced, 'All right, folks, Keith tells me we'll be at the Leeward Hotel in about two minutes.'

A weak cheer went up as he announced it. There was one comment of 'about bloody time, too' from George Robson, which Joe diplomatically ignored.

'You know the drill. Keith will help us unload the luggage then shift the bus while we check in. Today and tomorrow are yours to do as you like, but don't forget, tomorrow night, we have the Neil Diamond tribute show at the Winter Gardens, Saturday we have a day out in Bath, and on Sunday, it's one for the ladies with the Easter Bonnet Parade in the same Winter Gardens. I'll post notices in reception tomorrow morning, telling you where and what time we rendezvous.'

'Rendezvous?' asked Les Tanner. 'What are we doing, Murray? Launching an assault on Weston-super-Mare?'

Joe nodded. 'Yep, and you're the spearhead, which means you get shot first.' Joe clipped the microphone back on its rest and sat down again.

'You were a bit mild with Les,' Brenda noted.

'I'm tired,' Joe replied. 'George had it right.

This is too much of a journey for a mob like ours.'

Sheila yawned. 'Never mind the mob. It's too much of a journey for me. And it was Les's idea, if I recall. He and Sylvia spent a week in Burnham-on-Sea last summer, and they visited Weston for a day.'

The Grand Pier passed on the left and Brenda pointed to a large advertising hoarding. 'Oh, look, they're having an egg hunt here, too.'

Sheila and Joe followed her pointing finger to the electronic sign.

Charity Egg Hunt. Only 100 tickets available. £10 each. All proceeds to charity. Clifftop Park, Good Friday, 10.00am.

'They're having a similar thing in Wakefield, aren't they?' Joe asked.

'It's nationwide, Joe,' Sheila told him. 'There are about a hundred events going on all over the country. Each event hopes to raise one thousand pounds. It's tomorrow, so I imagine this one will be sold out.'

'What a way to raise money,' Joe grumbled 'I mean, why not just ask people to dip into their pockets?'

Brenda chuckled 'Hark at him. The last time you dipped into your wallet, you turned up two moths which had starved to death.'

'I do my bit,' Joe retorted. 'I employ you, don't I? Help keep you away from the men folk of Sanford.'

Brenda took the jibe in good part. 'There is so much I could do for you, Joe Murray. One night with me and…'

She trailed off under the warning glance from Joe. Sheila smiled thinly at them and Joe turned to watch the refurbished Winter Gardens pass on the right. He had no more interest in the view than he had in the charity egg hunt, but it was preferable to facing awkward questions.

Beyond the imposing, white front of the Winter Gardens, and its neatly trimmed, adjacent lawns, the road narrowed, with a view across the Bristol Channel to the left, and rows of flat-fronted hotels on the right. A public car park interrupted the endless line of buildings.

Once past it, Joe watched the white façade of the Leeward Hotel, its front patio devoid of life, streak by. 'Hey. You missed it.'

Keith shook his head. 'Have to turn round. If I pulled in on the right there, you lot would be getting off in the middle of the road.' He laughed. 'I think most of you need mowing down, but not while you're getting off my bus. The paperwork would be a nightmare.'

Joe grunted. 'Remind me again why you're still on my Christmas card list.'

A hundred yards further on, Keith stopped on the left and cautiously reversed his vehicle into a side road. Pulling out again, he cruised down to the Leeward entrance, stopped and opened the door.

'There you go,' Keith said as Joe grabbed his cagoule from the overhead rack. 'You can get off safely now, so don't forget my Christmas card.'

As usual, he and Joe were first off the bus, Keith to begin unloading the luggage, Joe to hurry ahead into reception to announce their arrival.

Reception was a generous description. Dashing in out of the rain, Joe found himself in a small space, the bar entrance to the right, the dining room to the left and the counter dead ahead, behind which sat a forty-something blonde wearing a pale green shirt which bore the hotel name across the breast pocket. The whole ambience reminded Joe more of a theatre box office than a hotel reception.

The Leeward boasted three floors of en suite rooms, many of which had been booked by the Sanford 3rd Age Club for the Easter weekend, and the moment he announced himself, he reappraised the hotel. The receptionist (Hazel according to her badge) was well prepared for them, a small stack of registration cards at the ready.

'If you bring your people in, Mr Murray, they can take their luggage into the bar, fill in their registration cards and I'll give them their keys as they come back.' She checked her memo pad. 'Some of your party were listed as elderly or disabled, so I've put them on the lower floors. Your bus driver is near you, up in the gods.'

'The amount of lip he gives me, he should be with God... permanently.' Joe turned to go out again. 'I'll wheel 'em in.'

In a matter of minutes, the bar was flooded with what, to Joe, was a familiar scene. Luggage stacked in the centre of the room, filling the small dance floor, people spread everywhere, completing their registration forms, while outside, Keith made a final tour of the bus to ensure no property had been left behind before moving it to the official coach park half a mile away.

The members began collecting their keys and slowly drifted from the bar, through a narrow door in the far left corner, which led, so Joe was assured, to the lifts. As usual, he was last to be attended, and it was fully half an hour before he collected the key to room 31, arranged to meet Sheila and Brenda in the bar, and then made his way to the lift, and up to the third floor.

Small, a little cramped, yet comfortable was Joe's first impression. A three-quarter bed giving him room to spread out when he slept, a tiny bath/shower/toilet, a single wardrobe, and a small settee alongside which was an occasional table upon which he could set up his laptop computer. The latter furniture stood beneath the only window, which he discovered looked out over the rear of the hotel. Through it, he could see an extension to the building which, he assumed, housed more rooms in its two floors. Beyond that was a small yard in which was parked a silver-grey 4x4, its polished bodywork gleaming in the dull, afternoon light.

'The room'll do, Joe,' he told himself as he hung his clothing in the wardrobe.

Ten minutes later, in the bar, Sheila concurred with his opinion. 'Not the standard we're used to, Joe, but it's cosy and comfortable.'

'Good value for Easter weekend,' Joe said. He checked his watch. 'A bit early for booze. I'll get a cup of coffee. You two want anything?'

'Just a cup of tea, Joe,' Sheila said.

Brenda smacked her lips. 'Campari and soda, Joe.' She grinned. 'It's never too early for drinkies.'

Joe glanced across at the bar. There was no one waiting for service and no one serving. On this side of the bar sat a large, muscular man, his head buried in a magazine dedicated to off-roading. Joe crossed the room, leaned on the bar, looked around, and looked over the bar.

'Are they open, do you know?' he asked of the man on the bar stool. Without waiting for an answer, he leaned over the bar and looked around again, as if expecting to find someone underneath. 'Shop,' he called.

The man on the stool stood, revealing himself to be a head taller than Joe. Huge arms, with bulging biceps, hung from strapping, square shoulders. Worn loose and outside his denims, his short-sleeved shirt hid his abdomen, but despite a small bulge, Joe guessed it would be solid and muscular.

He dropped his magazine on the bar, moved through the door to the lifts, and reappeared behind the bar a moment later.

Amusement twinkled in his dark brown eyes. 'What can I do for you, squire?'

Slightly taken aback, Joe took a moment to recover. 'I, er, oh, right. One tea, one coffee, and any danger of a Campari and soda?'

'Coming right up.' He turned away and placed a small metal jug under the catering-model coffee maker. While the machine bubbled and slurped away, he prepared cups on a tray, took down a small wine glass, and pressed it to the Campari optic.

'Sorry about that,' Joe said while he waited. 'Wasn't giving you any stick. I didn't realise you worked here.'

'Just taking five minutes while I can, mate,' the man replied. The machine stopped gurgling, and he poured the frothy coffee into a cup, placed it on a saucer and put it on the tray. Then he took a metal teapot and filled it with boiling water. Snapping the cap from a small soda, he put that on the tray too and passed the whole lot onto the bar. 'There you go, me old mate. You paying or do you want me to add it to your bill?'

'Stick it on the slate, will you? I'll settle up Monday. Room thirty-one.' Joe put his wallet back in his pocket. 'I should have guessed who you were.' He nodded at the man's magazine. 'Reading about off-roading, and I saw your 4x4 parked in the back yard.'

The barman pointed to a photograph pinned up behind the bar. It was the vehicle Joe had seen from his window. 'My pride and joy. It's what this—' he gestured upwards at the hotel, 'is all about.' He offered his huge hand. 'Freddie Delaney. Mein host, and that was my lady wife, Hazel, you met in reception.'

Joe shook it and found his gnarled fingers buried in the massive paw. 'Joe Murray. Owner of the Lazy Luncheonette, Sanford, and chair of the Sanford 3rd Age Club.'

Freddie beamed. 'So this mob are your responsibility are they, Joe?'

'They're not a bad lot.' Joe grinned slyly. 'They usually leave their flick knives and bike chains at home, and pack the condoms instead.'

'Bitta bed hopping, eh? That's what I like to hear.'

This time Freddie laughed and Joe began to warm to the genial giant.

An irritated Brenda crossed the floor and took the tray from Joe. 'We're getting thirsty.'

'Freddie, meet one of my managerial assistants, Brenda Jump. Brenda, this is Freddie Delaney. He owns this place.'

'Pleased to meet you, Freddie. Don't let Joe monopolise your attention. You'll never get any work done otherwise.'

'Take no notice,' Joe advised as Brenda walked off with the tray. 'So, Freddie, what do you recommend for a wet weekend in Weston-super-Mare?'

'Forecast says it's gonna brighten up from tomorrow artnoon. So what can you do between now and then? Lemme see...' Freddie's clear brow creased. 'There's a Neil Diamond lookalike at the Winter Gardens tomorrow night. He comes highly recommended.'

'Already got tickets, buddy.'

'Oh. Right. How about the great Easter egg hunt, then?' Freddie gestured to a leaflet pinned to the wall on Joe's left. 'Clifftop Park, tomorrow morning, ten o'clock. Only a hundred places available.'

'Yeah, the girls were on about it when we came in along the prom. There's supposed to be hundreds of events going on all over the country, isn't there? I know there's one in Wakefield, not far from where we live. This one'll be sold out, won't it?'

'Last I heard there were still some places available. Same with the Easter Bonnet Parade at the Winter Gardens on Sunday afternoon. You might have to look sharp if you're gonna get your lady friends in on them, mind.'

Joe dug out his wallet again. 'You got any tickets?'

'Don't work like that, Joe. Take yourself along the prom to Regent Street, opposite the Grand Pier. Walk up there, you'll come to the Weston Carrot—'

'The Weston Carrot?' Joe interrupted.

Freddie laughed again. 'It's a piece of functional artwork, they reckon. Tall thing, huge spire on the top. Looks like a carrot. Well, so they say. You can't miss it. At the bottom it's a bus shelter, newsagents and the local tourist centre. They'll sell you tickets for both events there. Cost you a tenner a ticket, mind, but it all goes to charity.'

Joe pointed to his companions. 'It'll cost *them* a tenner a ticket.'

* * *

'I dunno about a carrot,' Joe said. 'Looks more like a turnip to me.'

Standing almost eighty feet high, it was impossible to miss the *Silica*, the site's proper name. Shaped like a beehive at the bottom, its spire, circled with metal rings at regular intervals, tapered to a fine point at the top. Its pale grey colouring was what had prompted Joe's remark, made as they ambled along Regent Street towards the structure.

The Silica stood in a part-open area known as Big Lamp Corner – according to Sheila, reading from her guide book as they walked along. 'It's street art. Designed to improve the local environment.'

'How does sticking an eighty foot turnip in the middle of the street improve things?' Joe wanted to know.

'It's a focal point, Joe,' Brenda explained. 'A meeting place. If you had a date, you could arrange to meet at the Silica... or carrot... or even the turnip, if you like. You'd be sure to use some of the shops and cafes nearby, wouldn't you, and that's good for business, and aren't you the one who's always saying good business is good for the town?'

Joe could see what she meant. The area immediately around the Silica was an open triangle lined with shops and cafes, and along the sidewalk were several free-standing market stalls. Above them a banner fluttered in the wind. *Weston-super-Mare Easter Street Market*. As they neared, Joe saw that the market ran off along another street to the left.

'Tell you what,' Brenda suggested to Sheila, 'let's get the tickets for the two competitions, then we can have a wander along the market and pick up the bits to make our Easter bonnets.'

In the act of lighting a cigarette, Joe paused and stared at her, his eyes wide with disbelief. 'If you think I'm making an Easter bonnet, you've another think coming.'

'You can join the great egg hunt, though,' Sheila said.

'I can think of better ways of spending my time on a Good Friday morning than looking for chocolate eggs in a rainy park.'

'You don't know it will rain,' Brenda objected as they arrived at the tourist centre.

After some negotiation and more nagging, Joe conceded defeat and paid for three entries to the Great Easter Egg Hunt and two entries for the Easter Bonnet Parade.

'That's stretched the plastic close to breaking point,' he complained as they came back out onto the street. 'Fancy a cuppa? Only you'll have to pay, cos I'm broke.'

'Where's me violin?' Brenda joked.

'Later, Joe,' Sheila said. 'We need bonnets and bits and pieces to stick on them.'

'I've a suggestion,' he said. 'Buy a model cow, call it Joe, and label it 'cash cow'.'

'Shut up, Joe,' they said in chorus.

They ambled along the side street, checking the stalls on both sides. A sweet stall reminded Joe that he had not bought an Easter egg for his nephew's son, so he rang the Lazy Luncheonette.

'Lee, it's Joe.'

'Hello, Uncle Joe.'

'Listen, lad, I forgot to get an Easter egg for

Danny. Take money from the till and get him one from Patel's next door.'

'Will comb, Uncle Joe.'

'Wilco, you idiot,' Joe muttered as he cut the connection.

Ambling along the street, the two women bought identical hats of fake straw, and then began to gather the paper flowers, fluffy toys and plastic models they would need to decorate them.

'We need to be different,' Brenda said.

'I'm going for flowers,' Sheila agreed.

'And I'm going for livestock,' Brenda said.

'And I'm going for a pint,' Joe chipped in. 'I'll be in the pub over there.' He pointed to the dark-painted front of the Sword & Shield Inn along the street.

A black-haired woman, her stall displaying a vast range of Easter eggs in attractive, multi-coloured packaging, was shouting abuse at another woman, whom Joe took to be a customer. Above the stall a homemade banner read, *Ginny's Sweets*.

On closer inspection, he recognised the second woman right away. Swathed in a white anorak, middle-aged, her hair a shock of red, carrying a large handbag over one arm, and a large, boxed Easter egg clutched under the other, she was the same person who had crossed so carelessly in front of their bus. She appeared to show the same degree of disinterest in the stallholder's shouts as she had in Keith's annoyance.

The same could not be said of the passing shoppers, who watched with interest at the stallholder's increasing vehemence.

'D'you hear me? Clear off. And don't you come near me again.'

The redhead paused, turned, and stared back at the stallholder. 'That's the trouble with people like you. You don't know when someone's trying to do you a favour.' She turned again and continued walking away.

Under normal circumstances, Joe was as inquisitive as any other passer-by, but the incessant rain prompted Joe to ignore the argument and he crossed the street putting himself between the furious stallholder and the redhead for just a few seconds. As he did so, something hit him on the shoulder with a splat! Chocolate and cream spread across his cagoule and his left cheek.

The redhead turned, saw what had happened and cackled madly. The stallholder, whom Joe took to be Ginny, hurried out, and for a moment Joe thought she was after the redhead, but instead, she came to him.

'I'm so sorry. I wasn't aiming at you, but that cow.' She pointed indignantly at the redhead, who stuck up two fingers, then carried on walking away.

'It was a bloody rotten shot,' Joe grumbled, pulling out his handkerchief and wiping the chocolate and cream from his cheek.

'I've made an awful mess of your coat.'

With a grimace, Joe angled his head so he could peer down at his left shoulder. The pale blue cagoule was smeared with a nasty mess from the cream egg. Ginny made an effort to clean it up as

Sheila and Brenda joined them.

Brenda grinned. 'Tsk. I've told you before about hassling women in the street, Joe.'

'All I was doing was walking along,' he protested.

Ginny glanced at the two women, and eyed the wedding ring on Sheila's left hand. 'It was my fault, not your husband's.'

Sheila frowned. 'He's not my husband.'

Ginny transferred her attention to Brenda, who quickly denied any ties. 'He's not mine, either. We just look after him cos it's better than leaving him wandering the streets.'

'Sod off, you two.' Joe concentrated on the stallholder. 'There are ways and means of handling awkward customers, Mrs...'

'Virginia Nicholson. Most folk call me Ginny. And it's Ms, not Mrs. It's my stall, and she wasn't a customer. She's... well, let's just say we had a disagreement.'

'I'm Joe Murray, and these are my friends Sheila Riley and Brenda Jump. I have disagreements with people in my café, Ginny, but I don't throw pies at them.'

'Only because his pies are so stale, he'd probably kill them,' Brenda put in with another broad smile.

'I really must remember to get you to work on my public profile, Brenda.'

Before they could be sidetracked any further, Ginny said, 'I'll pay for your jacket cleaning.'

'Don't worry about it,' Joe said. 'Laundry is tax-deductible in catering.'

'Are you sure?'

Joe smiled into her concerned blue eyes. He guessed her to be in her early forties, a good ten years younger than him. A spreading waistline hinted that she probably dipped into her stock more than she should, but he nevertheless found her attractive, and he noticed the lack of jewellery on her hands.

'There's no harm done, but if you want to make amends, we'll be in the bar of the Leeward Hotel this evening. You can buy me a pint.'

Ginny appeared relieved. 'I'll see if I can make it.'

Chapter Two

Having spent his entire life in catering, no matter where the Sanford 3rd Age Club stayed, Joe's initial concentration was on the food.

'I run a pit stop for truckers and shoppers,' he would say, 'but that doesn't mean I don't know my onions when it comes to food.' The pun was intentional and backed up by his college diplomas in catering, or food technology as it had become known.

The dining room, a long, narrow annexe added to the rear of the Leeward Hotel, was cramped, leading Joe to the suspicion that Hazel and Freddie Delaney were determined to cram in as many bodies as possible. Sitting down to dinner on the first evening, along with Sheila, Brenda, Les Tanner and Sylvia Goodson, he nevertheless found the pork loin steaks excellent.

'And perfectly complemented with a glass of Chateau John Smith's,' he chortled as he drank his glass of bitter.

'Ever the connoisseur, Murray,' said Tanner.

'And how long has the Town Hall canteen been serving peppered venison in red wine and rosemary? I know good food when I taste it, Les, and I know good ale when I drink it.'

The thinly masked antagonism between Joe and Les had a long history, and it was largely superficial, but the food and ambience mellowed them almost to the point of conviviality, leaving the three ladies to lead the conversation.

'Brenda and I are going in for the Easter Bonnet Parade,' Sheila declared.

'So am I,' Sylvia said. 'And Julia Staines has bought a hat and the trimmings to go on it.'

'Are you tackling the Great Egg Hunt in Clifftop Park, too?' Brenda wanted to know.

Sylvia, a hypochondriac fusspot in Joe's opinion, shook her head. 'The forecast is for rain, and with my arthritis and my diabetes, I don't think it would be wise to wander around looking for Easter eggs. That's what we agreed, isn't it, Les?'

Joe concentrated on his meal while Les, whose relationship with Sylvia was one of the worst-kept secrets in Sanford, agreed. 'I know it's for charity, and all,' said the captain, 'but charity must have its limits. I felt it would do no good Sylvia putting herself at risk in order to do good for others.'

'Joe's taking part,' Sheila pointed.

'Now there you do surprise me, my dear,' Tanner said, eager to goad Joe again. 'I've always felt that when it comes to charity, Murray believes in starting and finishing at home.'

'Now, Les,' Sylvia chided him. 'I happen to know Joe does more than his share for good causes.'

'Thank you, Sylvia,' Joe replied. 'If nothing else, Les, I pay my taxes to keep you in the Town Hall where you can't do any real harm.'

The ping-pong game of mild insult, carried along by the banter of the three women, took them through a selection of desserts, and coffee, before they followed the rest of their fellows, leaving the dining room in small groups, to cross reception into the bar.

It seemed to Joe that the Sanford 3rd Age Club were the only residents, and for a brief moment he felt sorry for Freddie and Hazel. Running a business this size, he was certain they would need more than the seventy or so third-agers from Yorkshire to profit from the Easter holiday, especially considering the generous discount Joe had managed to negotiate.

The last time Joe noticed the small, wooden dance floor, it had been buried under the STAC luggage. Now it was clear, and in one corner of the room was a hi-fi set up and an amplifier. 'Entertainment,' he commented.

'The brochure did say there's live entertainment throughout the Easter holidays, and a disco on Sunday night,' Sheila reminded him.

'In that case, I need a drop of Campari to lubricate my dancing legs.' Brenda smacked her lips. 'Your shout, Joe.'

'It's always my shout.'

Sylvia and Tanner joined the Staineses on the far side of the room near the inner exit to the accommodation. Sheila and Brenda secured a table by the window, away from the hi-fi equipment, from where they could look out on a grey, rainy night settling on Weston-super-Mare. Across the half mile of sea, the lights of the pier could be seen barely breaking through the gloom and in the background, the darkening sky remained turgid and colourless.

Leaving the two women to sort out seating, Joe crossed to the bar where Freddie, Hazel and an additional barman were rushed off their feet filling the STAC members' orders.

'With you as fast as I can, Joe,' Freddie assured him.

'No rush, mate. I know my lot. They may be slow on their feet, but there's no crowd faster when it comes to shifting ale.'

Stood alongside him, Mort Norris took exception. 'You're a fine one to talk. Always first off the bus.'

'I have to be,' Joe retorted. 'I have to prepare these poor sods—' He gestured at the bar staff, '— for you lot.'

After serving one or two more, Freddie finally made it to Joe, much to Mort's annoyance.

'I was before him,' Mort complained.

'Yes, but I look thirstier than you.'

Freddie smiled. 'What is it, Joe?'

'Half of bitter, gin and tonic and a Campari and soda.'

'Ice and lemon?'

'Yes, but not in the beer. I—'

A shout from Hazel at the other end of the bar cut Joe off.

'Bitter's gone. Fresh barrel, Freddie.'

The landlord gave Joe a wan smile. 'Sorry, mate. Five minutes.'

Taking a large, open-ended wrench from the shelves behind him, Freddie disappeared through a rear door.

'I dunno what you're grinning at,' Joe said to Mort. 'You drink bitter, too.'

'Yes, luv?' Hazel said to Mort.

With a superior smile at Joe, Mort ordered, 'A pint of Guinness and a port and lemon, please.'

Several minutes later, Joe joined his two companions by the window while a forty-something man came in through the doors carrying a guitar and a case which they soon learned was filled with microphones, CDs and several bundles of cable.

'I like this place,' Brenda declared.

'Wait until he starts playing Black Sabbath,' Joe suggested.

'My Peter had a thing about Black Sabbath. He rather liked that heavy metal, er…'

'Racket?' Joe suggested when Sheila trailed off.

Brenda giggled. 'Be a bit of a bugger if he starts paying Neil Diamond.'

'Why? I like Neil Diamond.'

'Yes, Sheila, so do I, but we are going to see a Neil Diamond tribute show tomorrow night.'

'Oh. Yes. I see what you mean.'

They need not have worried. By the time Eddie Carson was set up and ready, it was dark outside, but the inclement weather soon faded while he ran through a first spot that began with Jeff Beck and ended with Lionel Ritchie, backing music coming through his hi-fi, which he augmented with his guitar.

He stepped down just after nine, promising to return when he had 'oiled' his vocal cords, and Joe returned to the bar for refills.

He stood at the opposite end this time, waiting for Hazel to serve him. Leaning forward, holding out his money, shouldering George Robson to one side, he glanced along the bar, and saw Ginny Nicholson at the far end talking to Freddie. He made an effort to attract her attention, but instead, managed to draw Hazel to him.

'Yes, Joe?'

'Oh, er, sorry,' he apologised. 'Miles away, then. Half of bitter, Campari and soda, gin and tonic, ice and lemon with the shorts.'

While Hazel pulled his drinks, Joe again glanced along the bar. Freddie was ignoring the crowds clamouring for drink, leaving it all to his wife and the barman. The big, cheery man was gone. Freddie's face was a picture of concern while he talked earnestly with Ginny.

People and their motives had always been a puzzle to Joe, and he freely admitted that he did not always handle them well. But he could not be fooled; body language and his keen sense of observation told him when others had problems, when others had encountered sudden change in their lives. He did not know which it was in the case of Ginny and Freddie, and while he had never seen Ginny anything but angry, it was obvious that something had tipped the scales for the landlord.

'You need more help,' he said to Hazel when she delivered his drinks. He nodded towards her husband.

She took his money and smiled at him. 'I'll kick him where he won't dare show his mum.'

Joe returned to the table and related the tale to Sheila and Brenda. 'If I didn't know better, I'd swear there was something between Freddie and Ginny.'

'How do you know there isn't?' Brenda asked finishing off her first drink and sipping at the second.

'With his wife stood not ten feet away?' Joe shook his head. 'I know Freddie's a big 'un, a bit like our Lee, but I'll bet that Hazel can go some if you wind her up the wrong way.'

'He does have a point, Brenda. Joe, have you ever considered the possibility that, erm…'

'Yes?' He prompted Sheila.

'It's none of your damned business.'

Joe took the frothy head off his beer. 'I was only commenting.'

At the bar, Hazel had a quiet word with Freddie, he concluded his conversation with Ginny, giving her a warm smile, and she turned away, holding a glass of what looked like vodka in her hands. Her gaze traversed the room, passed Joe and his companions, then tracked back to them. She left the bar and crossed the room to join them with a smile.

'Here I am,' she announced cheerfully. 'Ready to buy you that drink.'

Joe laughed, and reaching to the next table, drew up a chair for her. 'No, no. I was only kidding. Anyone buys the drinks round here, it's me.'

'But your jacket was a mess.'

'There was no harm done, Ginny,' Brenda

said. 'We cleaned him up when we got back here.'

'I feel so terrible about it, too. That bitch.' Her features darkened.

'The bitch in question being the redhead?' Joe asked. 'What was her name again?'

Ginny shook her head. 'I have several names for her, but I'm not gonna tell you who she is. All I will say is, if you see her, keep your distance. She's bad news, that one. I was just telling Freddie about it.'

Brenda gave Joe a look which said, "you see". 'Yeah, I noticed you talking to him. I tried to attract your attention, but you were deep into the tale and didn't notice.'

'Sorry.' She smiled. 'We go way back, me and Freddie and Hazel, and you know how it is when you haven't seen someone for a while. We were busy catching up.'

Joe doubted it, but elected not to say so.

Ginny swallowed a mouthful of her drink. 'So, what you folks doing down here? Easter holiday is it?'

Joe spent several minutes explaining the principle of the Sanford 3rd Age Club and their respective roles in it. At the end of his little lecture, Ginny was suitably impressed.

'I think that's damn nice of you, looking after a load of crumblies.'

'Crumblies?' Joe was so astonished, he almost dropped his glass. He waved at the room with his free hand. 'Lemme tell you something, Ginny. You're surrounded by the biggest set of born again teenagers, sex and beer mad thugs, you're likely to meet this side of a Hell's Angels' convention.'

'Crumbling they are not,' Brenda agreed.

Sheila tittered. 'Except for Sylvia Goodson.'

'And Alma Norris.'

The two women collapsed into fits of giggles.

'You'll have to excuse 'em, Ginny. They're in the early stages of senility.'

'Well, if they're all as fit as you reckon, maybe they should be out on the Great Egg Hunt in Clifftop Park, tomorrow.'

'We will be there,' Sheila assured her. 'And so will Joe, but we had to twist his arm—'

'And his wallet,' Brenda interrupted. 'He's too tired and too tight, y'see.'

Ginny laughed. 'Well, I hope you score plenty of eggs. But I'm warning you, they won't be easy to find.'

'And how would you know that?' Joe asked.

'Because I'm supplying them,' she replied. 'My bit for charity, you know. More than that, I have to be in Clifftop Park at half past eight tomorrow morning to hide them.'

* * *

Joe arrived promptly for breakfast at 8.00am, only to learn that it was not served until 8.30.

'Sorry, mate, but the sign is up on the wall,' Freddie said as he trucked a stack of boxed Easter eggs in through the front door.

'Not your fault,' Joe confessed. 'Mind you, I thought it was quiet up on the landing. I know my lot. There's no holding 'em back at feeding time.'

Joe rolled a cigarette and eyed the Easter eggs. He glanced outside where a lorry stood at the kerbside, the driver stacking more Easter eggs up at its rear. 'So what's with all the chocolate?'

'For you lot, innit?' Freddie replied, stretching across his barrow to open the dining room door.

Joe hurried across to hold it open for him. 'We're third agers, Freddie, not kids. We don't need Easter eggs.'

Freddie pushed past him into the dining room where staff were laying out the tables. He paused to face Joe, his large face split into a smile. 'A deal's a deal, my old chum. When we put the package together, we aimed it at families, and Hazel decided that we'd throw in a small Easter egg for every guest at Sunday lunch. Mind you, you're not the only crowd we've got in this weekend. We have families, too. In fact, a few more are due in today. You're all getting an Easter egg whether you want one or not. If you don't want it, give it to the charity do at the Winter Gardens.' He smiled again. 'Sorry, Joe, I'd like to stay and chat, but I gotta another eight dozen to get off the lorry, and I need to get these into the cold room.'

Joe tucked his tobacco tin back in his pocket. 'Let me give you a hand. I'm used to it.'

'I dunno, mate. Health and safety, you know…'

'Gar. Don't be so soft, man. I've been doing it forty years.'

'All right.'

Joe followed Freddie through the dining room,

into the kitchen, where, to the angry complaints of the deputy head chef, the staff were busy preparing the one hundred and something breakfasts.

'Give 'em some,' Joe encouraged the chef. 'I like to see a man who knows how to run a kitchen.'

'Like a busman's holiday for you, then,' the chef replied.

Joe grinned. 'You need a hand kicking their backsides, let me know.'

Ahead of him, Freddie opened the walk-in cold room and trucked the Easter eggs through.

Right behind him, Joe pointed out, 'You don't need to keep the chocolate chilled, you know.'

'I know, but we ain't got nowhere else to store 'em.'

Freddie ranged himself alongside the barrow, Joe stood by the shelves, and as Freddie tossed them to him in pairs, he stacked them in rows just above his head. As he placed the last pair, Freddie backed out of the cold room and the lorry driver entered with another truckload.

As fast as he packed away one load, another appeared, and it was not until the job was done, while Freddie checked the delivery note and signed for it, that Joe had time to look around.

Aside from the chocolate eggs, it was a sight so familiar to him that he could have been transported back to the Lazy Luncheonette. Around the cramped area were stacked large cartons which he recognised as catering sized cans of baked beans and processed peas, boxes of pre-packed bacon and ranges of eggs. When he checked the chest freezer, he found pork, beef, lamb, and a full range of frozen vegetables. On the shelves were boxes he recognised and containing individual portions of butter, vegetable spread, jam and marmalade, and in one corner was a giant Easter egg, its ruffled gold foil wrapping glinting irregularly in the interior light.

'Home from home?' Freddie asked.

The question snapped Joe out of his reverie. 'Hmm. What? My cold store isn't as big as this, but I reckon as a truckers' caff, I turn my stock over faster than you do.' He pointed at the large Easter egg. 'Which lucky kid gets that?'

Freddie frowned. 'Dunno. That's my bit for charity.'

Freddie ushered him out of the cold room, switched off the light and closed the door behind them.

'So what is this charity thing?' Joe asked as they made their way back through the dining room. 'You mean that thing up at Clifftop Park?'

'Nah, mate. The great egg hunt is only one event.'

They made their way outside and lit cigarettes.

'There's the Easter Bonnet Parade, too,' Freddie went on. 'That's on Sunday.'

'The girls are going in for it,' Joe told him.

'Yeah? Well good luck to 'em. As part of the appeal, the organisers are collecting chocolate, sweets, soft toys and stuff, for distribution. That's today and tomorrow. Then after the Easter Bonnet Parade on Sunday afternoon, the whole lot will be shipped off to hospitals and orphanages. The kids are supposed to get it all on Easter Monday.'

'Well let's hope Sanford gets some of it. Keep the thieving little swine outta my place for a day or two.'

Freddie laughed. 'Get a lot of hassle from 'em, do you?'

'Only when my back's turned.' Joe drew in a lungful of smoke and expelled it in a hiss. He gazed sourly at the rain. 'It can't always be like this here.'

'Great this place when the sun shines, Joe,' Freddie told him. 'Best move I ever made coming down here.'

Joe was surprised. 'You're not a local then?'

'Nah, mate. I'm from Gloucester originally. Came down here about five, six years ago. Good move, you know. I've always worked in bars, landed a job here when Hazel was on her own. She needed a bar and cellarman. We worked together for a good while, then we sort of got it together. Married three years ago.'

'It turned out well on all fronts for you, then.'

Freddie watched the traffic passing in the rain, but the glazed look in his eyes told Joe he wasn't concentrating on the view. 'She's the boss, Joe, but I have to say she's the best thing that ever happened to me. Keeps me in check, keeps me well fed and well looked after.' His face split into a broad grin. 'And she bought me my four by four. She's a good girl. The best.'

Joe had his doubts. He knew how sour relationships could turn when a couple not only lived together but worked together, too. 'Good on you, Freddie,' he encouraged. 'Now. Tell me how we get to this Clifftop Park.'

Freddie pointed to the right. 'You follow the headland round, and then turn inland. It's not far, but take my tip and book a taxi. There's a steep hill from the seafront that's like trying to climb Everest.'

Chapter Three

Clifftop Park sat, appropriately, on the north cliff. A designated country park, densely wooded with footpaths running in all directions through it, when the taxi ran along the access road, Sheila speculated that it would be a wonderful place to pass a relaxing summer's afternoon.

'Not so nice on a wet Good Friday morning,' Joe grumbled.

'Oh, do be quiet, Joe,' Sheila berated him. 'Just think of the good we're doing. All over the country, thousands of people like us are about to set off on the Great Egg Hunt.'

'Yeah. Hard to imagine there could be that many idiots in the country, isn't it?'

It was the only thing Joe had found to complain about since his arrival. The previous evening's entertainment and relaxed ambience had been augmented by a superb breakfast at the Leeward before they called the taxi for the ten-minute journey to the park. It seemed to him that Weston-super-Mare was determined to tackle and beat his inherent skill at griping, and although he kept the thought to himself, he was happy to be here, happy to be with his friends, more than content to be away from the hectic world of the Lazy Luncheonette.

The only downer was the weather. The rain had not abated overnight, and with the church clocks reading 9.45, the sky remained dull, leaden, overcast, delivering constant, if light rain.

The taxi dropped them at the main gate, where the car parking spaces were already filled. A security man, wearing a navy blue coat and high-visibility vest over his chocolate brown uniform, took their tickets and let them through for the short walk into the park and its large, wooden pavilion.

Painted white with dark green edging, it was a long, low building, surrounded by woods on three sides, fifty metres or so from the pavilion, and between the building and the trees was an open area of finely mown grass, sodden underfoot, squelching audibly as they made their way to the pavilion.

'Ideal for summer picnics,' Brenda said.

'Another one,' Joe complained. 'Do I need to remind you it's not summer. It's early spring and pi—'

'Language,' Brenda interrupted.

'I was going to say piddling down.'

A crowd had gathered before the pavilion, a hundred or so people most clad in wet-weather clothing, many sporting umbrellas, all focussed on the raised deck of the building, where local dignitaries, one of them the Mayor, his official station in life announced by his chain of office, were gathered. To one side of them was a trestle table stacked with small, wicker baskets.

Other people followed them in, everyone crowding to hear the official announcements. With the time at 9.55, one of the officials took centre stage.

Sheltering under an umbrella, a microphone in

his hand, he announced, 'Good morning ladies and gentlemen, and welcome to the Weston-super-Mare Great Egg Hunt, just one event of a hundred or so going on around the country. My name is Robert Quigley, and I'm the local organiser for Giving GB, the charity which has arranged all the events. I'm not going to bore you with the details of those charities we support. You can find a list of them on our website. Instead I'm going to spell out the few rules pertaining to today's event.' Quigley waved at the woods around them. 'Ms Virginia Nicholson, known to the local townsfolk for her sweet stall on the street markets, has donated two hundred Easter eggs to the hunt. She was here first thing this morning, hiding them in the woods.' He held up a canned air horn. 'When the siren goes, you have one hour to find as many as you can, and those you do find, you keep. The eggs are hidden on all three sides in the first thirty metres of the woodland. You'll know when you come to the boundary because it is roped off and there are no hidden eggs beyond the rope.' He gestured at the trestle table. 'For those of you who didn't bring a bag to hold your eggs, we have baskets available at one pound each. All proceeds, naturally, go to our nominated charities. When the time is up, I will sound two blasts on the air horn. Doubtless, you'll find it thirsty work, and there will be tea, coffee and soft drinks available in the pavilion when the hunt is over.' Quigley's face became slightly more serious. 'Under health and safety regulations, we are obliged to have an emergency signal. If you hear the horn sound three times in succession, it means we have some kind of emergency, and you should vacate the woods, and return to the pavilion.' Quigley looked up into the dull skies. 'I can't see us getting a forest fire today, but should an emergency arise, security officials will come into the woods to check that everyone is on their way back.' He smiled again. 'And now I'd like to hand over to his worship the Mayor to formally get the hunt under way.'

There followed a two-minute address from the mayor. Joe sensed the restlessness of the crowed, eager to get away from the local politician.

'I think I'll have one of those baskets,' Sheila said, while His Worship extolled the charitable virtues of local businesses who had given their wholehearted support to the hunt. 'They'll make a nice souvenir.'

'Probably made of cardboard,' Joe said.

'So where will you put your eggs without one, Joe?' Brenda asked. 'And don't tell me it's where no woman would dare to look, because...' She trailed off under a warning glance from him.

The mayor finished his short speech, raised the air horn in his hand and, wincing in anticipation of the noise, pressed the cap.

People hurried off in all directions. Sheila and Brenda, along with a number of others, made for the trestle table, and soon the baskets and money were changing hands.

The man standing next to him, whose wife had hurried to buy a basket, nudged Joe. 'Your wife and her, er, friend seem to be entering into the spirit of the thing.'

'I wouldn't know,' Joe replied. 'My wife's in Tenerife. They're just my bits on the side.'

The man gawped and when his wife returned they wandered off to the right, occasionally glancing back as he related Joe's words to her.

Returning with a basket, which, as Joe had guessed, was made of stiffened cardboard, Brenda spotted the couple and asked, 'What's up with those two?'

'Dunno,' Joe lied. 'He seemed to think that you and Sheila are my wives, so I put him right.' Sheila joined them. 'Come on,' he urged. 'Let's go find some chocolate chuckies.'

* * *

Ferreting through the thick undergrowth, Joe poked into bushes with a long twig he had picked up when they entered the woods.

Several days of persistent rain had turned the undergrowth to mulch, smelling of decomposition. Even wearing gloves, they had learned that rooting through fern and bush was unhealthy, and Joe had quickly found broken branches for each of them.

Although the eggs were all wrapped in gaily coloured foil, the lack of light hampered their search. Up above, through the spring canopy of leaves and branches, there were glimpses of the sky, dull, leaden, turbulent and hanging with rain.

Sheila drifted off alone several yards to the right. Joe and Brenda continued working the left hand edge of the wood, close to the red rope strung around tree trunks, and Joe's complaints increased geometrically with every step he took. 'How long have we been at it?'

'Twenty minutes,' Brenda replied, parting the leaves of a large bush to glance at the ground beneath.

'And I've got one egg. It's cost me a tenner. I could have gone into Woolworths and bought it for three quid.'

'No you couldn't,' Brenda disagreed. 'Woolworths went bust years ago.'

'Patel's minimarket, then. In fact, I could probably have bought a dozen of them from the wholesaler for a tenner.'

'Shut up moaning, Joe, and think how much good your money's going to do for some chid.'

Joe pushed on, pressing aside a thicket of ferns. 'It'd do the kid more good if they sent him to the Lazy Luncheonette and I taught him how to work.'

'His air fare would cost you a fortune,' Brenda pointed out.

'How many have you found?'

'Two,' Brenda replied.

'See. You're already making a bigger profit than me. A hundred percent profit, as it happens. I paid the fees, so your outlay was nil.'

'Joe, I—'

Unwilling to take the debate any further, Joe abruptly changed the subject. With a furtive glance around to ensure Sheila was not in earshot, he asked, 'Have you said anything? You know. About us getting together more often?'

Brenda, too, checked to see if Sheila was

nearby, but she was several yards away, bending to check the ground under a low tree. 'No. Have you?'

'Have I hell as like. But you nearly gave the game away twice. Once on the bus yesterday, and just now, when we were at the pavilion.'

'I think she suspects, and really we should talk to her about it. We've been friends since we were children, Joe. I...' Brenda trailed off as Sheila hurried towards them, skirting thickets and bushes in a staccato dance. Under the hood of her light blue anorak, her face was white and they could see her shaking.

'Sheila?' Brenda asked. 'What is it?'

Her voice trembled as she replied. 'A woman. I think she's... I think she's dead. Joe...' she trailed off, appealing to him with eyes near to tears.

Joe instantly forgot his complaints. He hurried past Brenda and led them back along the track Sheila had taken. Brenda hung back, coming behind at a slower pace. Sheila, he knew, was stronger than Brenda. Brenda did not do death and dead bodies. He mentally prepared himself for the worst. Even Sheila, normally a stalwart, was distressed, and that filled his mind with images of badly decomposed corpses. As he rushed through the undergrowth, he felt his legs beginning to tremble.

Sheila stopped by a clump of bushes and pointed.

Joe half crouched and looked down. A lower leg, the calf bare, foot clad in dirty, white trainers, projected from under the bushes. He knelt and touched the foot above the ankle. Still warm, but he could feel no pulse. Peering under the bush, he could see the other leg, the knee bent, and above it, a dark skirt. He stood, put on his gloves, leaned forward and parted the shrubbery to look down on the woman's upper half. She wore a dark coat. Above it, her black hair was matted with blood.

Recognition rang through his head. He backed off and faced his companions. 'I think it's Ginny Nicholson. Her head's been caved in. Sheila, you and Brenda better get back to the pavilion, tell them to call the egg hunters back and get the police here.'

'What are you going to do, Joe?'

'I'll stay here and make sure no one disturbs the area.' Muttered voices reached them from a short distance away. 'You'd better get a move on.'

* * *

It took the women less than two minutes to get back to the pavilion where they outlined the problem to the organisers.

Quigley vacillated. 'Oh dear, this is most unfortunate. I do hope the hunters don't want their money back.'

Brenda glared. 'Are you for real, or did you train at the Joe Murray school of priorities? There is a dead woman out there. You need to get everyone out of the woods and get the law here.'

'What. Oh. Yes. Of course.' Quigley turned to the security chief. 'Can you get your people into the woods with megaphones, order everyone out? Don't tell them why. Just say it's an emergency. I'll telephone the police.'

The security chief hurried off to carry out the instructions.

'Joe has stayed with the body, Mr Quigley,' Sheila explained. 'He's quite experienced at this kind of thing.'

'He's a police officer, is he?' asked Quigley with obvious relief. 'Thank the lord of small mercies.'

'Joe, a cop?' Brenda smiled. 'Not likely. He runs a truck stop.'

Quigley blanched. 'What? Runs a—'

'Just ignore Brenda, Mr Quigley,' Sheila reassured him. 'Joe's niece is a Detective Sergeant with Sanford CID, and my late husband was a police inspector. We're familiar with the routines. Joe will ensure that nothing is disturbed until the police and their Scientific Support people get here.'

* * *

Back in the woods, the first inkling Joe had that things were moving was a triple blast on the air horn, followed by muttered noises from various megaphones as the security team made their way into the various areas of the forest.

As the security team neared his quarter, the message became clear. 'Ladies and gentlemen, please evacuate the woods. We have an emergency on our hands. Please return to the pavilion. The siren has been sounded three times. This is an emergency. Please return to the pavilion.'

Joe looked up. Through the canopy of trees he could make out the grey of the sky. Rain fell persistently and it had begun to soak his cagoule. Odd that he hadn't noticed it when he was busy hunting Easter eggs. He shivered and diagnosed that it was not entirely down to the chilly morning.

Looking straight ahead, he could barely make out the open grass lawns and, in the distance, the pavilion. He hoped that Sheila and Brenda wouldn't have too much trouble leading the police back to him. He wanted to be away from this forbidding little place quickly, back in the shelter of the pavilion with a cup of tea to warm his shaking insides.

A rustling sound came through the bushes immediately ahead of him. His hopes rose, but were promptly dashed when a security officer, easily identified by his dark brown uniform, appeared. It was too soon for the cops to get here.

'You need to get out quick sport,' said the young man.

'I can't.'

'Look, mate, there's some kind of emergency on. You—'

'I'm guarding the emergency,' Joe interrupted. 'I can't leave until the police get here.'

Beneath his straw hair, the younger man frowned. 'I don't understand.'

Joe stood to one side and gestured down with an open hand. The security man looked down and his pale features faded further. 'Oh Christ. Is she—

'Dead? Say it, son. There's nothing wrong with the word and no need to be melodramatic. Yes, she's dead. Her head has been stoved in. We found her, me and my two friends, and I need to stay put until the filth arrive.'

'I, er, I'm... I'm not sure I can...' He trailed off.

'Best thing you can do, lad, is get on with clearing the woods. I'll stay put to keep any nosy parkers away.'

'Yes. Er, right. That's what I'll do. I'll, er, I'll help get the people out of the woods.'

Obviously relieved, the security man hurried off and Joe found himself shivering once more, and silently willing the police to get a move on. He did not have long to wait. In less than five minutes he could hear the distant wail of sirens, and in his mind's eye, he imagined a convoy of police vehicles, their blue, emergency lights cutting through the drab daylight, hurtling along the path to the pavilion.

More minutes passed and at last he could see movement ahead of him. The breaking of bracken underfoot, and the rustling of bushes heralded the arrival of two uniformed officers, both wrapped up in high-visibility jackets.

'Right, sir,' said the elder policeman. 'Constable Tetlow, Avon and Somerset Constabulary. I believe you found the lady.'

'Sort of,' Joe said. 'Look, now that you're here, can I get off back to the pavilion. I need a cuppa.'

Taking out his notebook, Tetlow asked, 'You've disturbed nothing?'

It was as if he had not heard a word Joe said. 'That's why I've been stood here like a spare part for the last ten or fifteen minutes. To make sure nothing was touched.'

'Your name, sir?'

'Murray. Joe Murray. Listen—'

'And you're obviously not a local with an accent like that.'

'Sanford. West Yorkshire. Look—'

'Where are your staying, Mr Murray?'

'The Leeward. If you'd let me get a word in, I'm bloody freezing. I know the crack at murder scenes. I've... my niece is a CID officer. Can I leave you to look after things while I try and thaw out? I'm not going anywhere other than the pavilion.'

Tetlow finished his notes. 'All right, sir. Leave it with us but don't wander away from the area.'

Joe fumed. 'Do you speak English in this part of the world?'

'Sir?'

'Didn't I just say I wasn't going anywhere?'

'I'm sorry, Mr Murray, but there are procedures—'

'I'll be in the pavilion when you want a full statement,' Joe said, taking his turn to interrupt. With a nod, he walked off, treading the path the police had followed, out onto the expansive lawns, hurrying across the sodden grass, making for the large wooden hut opposite.

***

Sitting beneath the red glow of an ineffectual overhead heater, Joe was still shivering when the police, led by a woman in plain clothes, entered the busy pavilion half an hour later.

The place was crowded with hunters, organisers and security staff. At the rear of the room, the trestle table where tea, coffee and cakes were served, had become the social fulcrum. No one had yet been interviewed, and no one was permitted to leave. Some hunters were already becoming vocal on the matter.

'You're sure it was Ginny Nicholson, are you, Joe?' Sheila asked, returning from another visit to the tea table.

Joe clasped grateful hands around a cup. 'I didn't turn her over to take a look, if that's what you mean.' He shuddered at the memory of her battered skull. 'It certainly looked like her.'

'The very woman who hit you with a chocolate egg, yesterday, Joe.'

Joe scowled at Brenda's flippant remark. 'That probably makes me the prime suspect, then, huh?'

Brenda smiled again. 'Well, maybe whoever killed her had been hit by chocolate and cream himself.'

'Or herself,' Joe added and the women stared. 'Have you forgotten who she was arguing with? So what price it was that red-haired nutter? The one who crossed the road in front of our bus.' The announcement met with further gapes. 'Well they weren't getting on any too well, and she wasn't impressed by Ginny's screaming at her.'

The general level of chatter rose with the arrival of the police. The woman heading the team had a brief word with the organisers, then stood front and centre by the tea table.

'Ladies and gentlemen, if I could have your attention please.' She waited for the hubbub to die down then went on. 'I am Detective Chief Inspector Patricia Feeney, senior investigating officer in this matter. You're all probably aware, we have the body of a woman in the woods, and it does appear as if she has been murdered. My officers will take statements from you all. I'm sorry, but it will take some time, and I'm afraid we cannot allow anyone to leave until we have spoken to you.' Behind her, the uniformed men and women began to arrange themselves at trestle tables. 'My officers will call you by name. Once you've been spoken to, you will be free to leave.' Her eyes scanned the room. 'Is Mr Murray here, please?'

Conscious of all eyes turning on him, Joe half rose. 'I'm Joe Murray.'

Signalling another plain clothes officer to accompany her, she wove her way through the crowds, pulled up two chairs and sat with the three companions.

'This is Detective Sergeant Holmes, Mr Murray.'

Joe managed a thin smile. 'Not Sherlock, I hope.'

The sergeant grimaced. 'I get enough of that

at the station. My name is Neal Holmes.'

'Right. Good to meet you, Neal.'

'I take it you are Mrs Riley and Mrs Jump?' Feeney asked of the two women. When they had properly introduced themselves, the chief inspector went on. 'Constable Tetlow, the officer you met in the woods, Mr Murray, told me your niece is a CID officer in Sanford, West Yorkshire.'

'Detective Sergeant Craddock,' Joe told her.

'I already know,' Feeney replied. 'I spoke to her about ten minutes ago. That's how I knew your two lady friends were Mrs Riley and Mrs Jump.' Feeney paused to let Joe take in the information. 'Gemma, your niece, told me quite a bit about you. And you have a reputation for... how shall I put it...' The chief inspector groped for the correct word.

'Investigating?' Joe suggested.

'No. It's more like... well, I hesitate to use the word interfering, but—'

'You mean sticking my nose in.' Joe cut her off, and when Feeney nodded, he grunted. 'Did Gemma tell you that I also have a nasty habit of getting to the right answers before the police? Did she tell you about that idiot boss of hers who tried to nail me as a serial killer a couple of months back? And did she tell you that I sidelined him and got to the truth first?'

Feeney took his irritation in her stride. 'All very commendable. However, this is Avon and Somerset, Mr Murray, not West Yorkshire. Like any other police force, we are more than happy to listen to any information the public may be able to supply, but I want to make it clear that no matter what your reputation, I will not tolerate interference in my investigation.'

Joe held up his hands in a gesture of compliance. 'No. Hey. That's fine. We came here for the weekend, not to investigate a murder.' He dipped into his pockets, took out his tobacco tin and began to roll a cigarette. 'The dead woman looked like Virginia Nicholson to me. Was I right?'

'We can't confirm her identity yet,' Feeney replied. 'Not until her family have been informed and we have a positive identification from them.'

'No, no. Course not.' Joe sipped his tea again. 'Only, just so we can get all the nonsense out of the way before we go any further, Ginny threw a chocolate egg across the street yesterday and it hit me. But it didn't lead to any confrontation. In fact, she was with us in the bar of the Leeward last night. Isn't that right, girls?'

Sheila and Brenda confirmed the story.

'She threw an Easter egg at you and then you found her dead.'

'Joe didn't actually find her, Chief Inspector,' Sheila put in. 'I did.'

The police attention swung to her and they listened while she explained what had transpired in the woods. When she had finished, Feeney said, 'But Mr Murray was quite close by the scene all the time, wasn't he?'

Joe was about to protest, but Brenda got in first. 'We were together when we left the pavilion, Sheila drifted off alone, but Joe was with me from that point on. He didn't kill her.'

'And we've all three been together all morning,' Joe said in support, 'so if I bumped her off, it means we were all involved.'

'Getting back to yesterday, one wonders why she threw the egg at you in the first place,' Feeney said.

With an impatient sigh, Joe explained the circumstances leading to the incident, while Sergeant Holmes took notes.

'If you wanna look for anyone, you should dig up this redhead,' Joe concluded.

'We'll bear it in mind.' Feeney raised her hands and let them fall into her lap again in a gesture of finality. 'Thank you for your help, Mrs Riley, Mrs Jump, Mr Murray. I don't think we need detain you any longer. You look like you could do with a hot bath, Mr Murray.' She stood up, ready to leave. 'If there's anything more we need to know, we'll get to you at the Leeward.'

'Yeah, sure,' Joe agreed and put away his tobacco tin. 'Course, you'll have your people go through the woods and collect the remaining eggs, won't you?'

Feeney exchanged an irritated glance with Holmes, before concentrating on Joe. 'I beg your pardon?'

'Y'see, I looked when we found her, but I couldn't see any sign of Easter eggs. Now, we know that Ginny was planting two hundred eggs for this morning's hunt, cos that's what she told us, but where are they? Had she planted them all? If so, they're still out there. Now if I were you, I'd check on how many eggs the hunters have collected,' he waved at the room, 'then get people into the woods to find the rest, and add them all up.'

The chief inspector sat down again. 'And what would be the point?'

Tucking the rolled cigarette into his shirt pocket, Joe explained, 'There are two possibilities. It was an opportunist killing or it was planned. If it was opportunist, then what are the chances that she had planted all two hundred eggs when the killer came across her? If she hadn't, then it means the killer took the rest of them. Stealing a few chocolate eggs seems pretty poor reason for killing someone, if you ask me. If, on the other hand, it was a planned murder, it means the killer may have waited until she had finished planting the eggs. How did he get to that particular part of the woods without being seen and more important, how did he know Ginny would be right there? If it was planned, it means it was by someone who knew her and knew she would be there or in the vicinity. The only way you'll get a clue is by having your people get into the woods and collect the remaining eggs.'

Feeney's ears coloured slightly. 'Yes. Of course. It's obvious when you look at it that way. Well, I'll get my team onto it.'

'Here's another question you might ask,' Joe said, getting to his feet. 'What was Quigley doing letting the hunt go ahead when she hadn't come out of the woods?'

'Sorry?' Holmes asked. 'I'm not with you.'

Joe sighed. 'Ginny went into the woods this morning to plant two hundred Easter eggs. Right?' Joe waited for them to nod confirmation. 'I don't know how Quigley arranged it, but surely, the woman must have reported back to him to tell him the job was done. Now how did she do that if she was dead?'

Chapter Four

Back at the Leeward, while Joe went straight to his room to take a hot bath, Sheila and Brenda collected their Easter bonnets, found window seats in the bar, ordered coffee, and worked on their hats, occasionally looking out on the blustery, rainy weather.

'We've had better, sunnier Easter weekends,' Brenda commented, pressing a sprig of fake fern to her hat and examining the effect.

Sheila shuffled through an assortment of paper flowers. 'We've had worse ones, too. Remember a few years ago when Easter fell on April first? We woke up to four inches of snow in Sanford.'

'I remember.' Brenda held up a needle to the light and threaded it. 'Joe was out with the snow shovels in front of the Lazy Luncheonette, and then he came round, did my drive and yours, didn't he?' The needle threaded, she chuckled. 'Despite all his griping, he's a good-hearted soul, you know, and he always gets the worst of everything. This time, too. Turning up a body like that, volunteering to stand out there until the police arrived. Typical of him.'

Sheila's attention had wandered slightly, as she watched a woman struggle with an umbrella, but something in Brenda's wistful tones brought her back into the bar. 'Joe and the body? Well, he always did enjoy a good mystery, didn't he? Remember when we were in school? He was always in trouble for reading Agatha Christie or John Creasey instead of the set books. He probably wanted to get as much, er, evidence, for want of a better word, from the site this morning before the police took over.' She took out her glue, and began work on the flowers.

Fern pressed to the hat brim, Brenda began to sew. 'And he certainly put that chief inspector in her place, didn't he?' Her face became more serious. 'Sheila, there's, er, something I think you should know.'

'Oh yes?'

Sheila's brisk, business-like response confirmed that Brenda had got the tone, interested, serious but not quite grave, just right. Sheila was busy gluing the first flower, a pink carnation, to her hat, yet Brenda had no doubt she was giving most of her attention to the impending revelation.

'It's about his lordship and me. Well, really, it's none of your business, but we're the best of friends, the three of us, and I think you should know. I, er… oh dear. I'm not really sure how to put it.'

Sheila tittered. 'My friend, Brenda Jump, lost for words. That doesn't happen very often. Why not just say it straight, like you usually do?'

'Because it's more delicate than usual. It's… oh God, I really don't know how to say this.'

Sheila put down her hat and took a sip of coffee. 'You're trying to tell me that you and Joe spend the occasional night together.'

Brenda felt the colour rush to her cheeks. She too, put down her Easter bonnet and gazed fondly upon her best friend. Slowly, her stare softened and her face split into a broad grin. 'You never cease to surprise me, Sheila Riley. There you sit, looking as if butter wouldn't melt, but you spot everything and take it all so calmly. I thought you would be outraged.'

'Why should I be? As you pointed out, it's no concern of mine. If you're asking my opinion, I think it's a bad move, but only from the point of view that you have to work together, and remember how rough it was when Joe ran the Lazy Luncheonette with Alison.'

Brenda nodded, picked up her cup and gazed through the windows.

'It's been going on since Valentine's, hasn't it?' Sheila asked.

With one eye on the outside world, Brenda said. 'A lot longer than that, but since the day you and he were held at gunpoint by that nutter, we've been seeing more of each other. If you remember we all got roaring drunk that night. You included.'

Sheila picked up her bonnet and began work again. 'Relief,' she admitted. 'That was a very dangerous situation, and Joe behaved with commendable bravery.' She frowned. 'Even if he did break my Capo di Monte figure of *Pagliaccio*. It was natural to get drunk.'

Following suit, Brenda collected her hat, and sorted through her collection of soft toys. Choosing a rabbit, she pressed it into place on the right hand side of the hat and began to sew again. 'Not natural for you,' Brenda disagreed. 'I don't think I've seen you that blotto since your twenty-first birthday party. Anyway, we took you home in a taxi, but Joe was blathered, too, and I was seven sheets to the wind. We really don't know how it happened, but the next morning, Joe woke up in my bed. I mean, it's not the first time, but...'

'So you obviously...' Sheila trailed off, letting the suggestion hang.

With the rabbit sewn into place, Brenda sipped her coffee. 'The truth is, neither of us can remember anything about that night after dropping you off, and really, we only remember that because we must have done. I swore Joe to absolute secrecy, and he says he didn't want it broadcast all over Sanford. Anyway, a couple of days later, I invited him back after a session in the Miner's Arms, and this time we did.' Her ears burned an uncharacteristic pink. 'He's really quite, er, *sprightly* for a man his age, you know.'

Sheila disapproved light-heartedly. 'I don't know and I don't want to know, thank you.' She sipped her tea. 'How serious is it?'

Brenda gave a little snort of laughter that could have been lascivious or cynical. 'How serious do I ever get with men? I've been dating George Robson on and off for three years, but it's never amounted to more than the occasional one-night stand.' She shrugged. 'Joe and I are not serious, but in the last six weeks, we've spent more nights together than usual. Joe hasn't said as much, but I know he's not concerned for getting too involved either. It's still a bit of fun, Sheila. When we feel like it.'

Sheila held up her hat to judge the effect of

the two flowers she had pressed into place. With the slightly distracted air of one working on one item while talking about another, she repeated, 'As you said, it's none of my concern. Have either of you thought about the effect it will have on your working relationship?'

'So far, it hasn't,' Brenda replied. 'If it had, I'm sure you'd be the first to notice. I'm still working like a dog in the kitchen, and Joe is as grumpy as ever in behind the counter... even after he's had his legover.'

'Be careful, Brenda,' Sheila insisted as a dark grey Vauxhall saloon pulled up in front of the Leeward. 'I'd advise Joe to do the same. We don't want to sully friendships that go back as far as ours.'

'And talking of friendships,' Brenda said, determined to change the subject, 'here's a new one just blooming.' She nodded through the windows where Chief Inspector Feeney and Sergeant Holmes had just climbed out of the Vauxhall.

'It didn't sound very friendly at Clifftop Park,' Sheila commented. 'More like fresh enmity in the making.'

'She has an eye for Joe.' Brenda laughed, deliberately and garishly. 'And he'll charm her. You watch.'

* * *

'I thought we weren't going to deal with this bloke, ma'am,' Holmes ventured as he followed his chief through the large patio to the hotel entrance.

'Murray? We're not,' Feeney replied. 'But his niece did tell me he's known for his powers of observation. We're going to test them, Sergeant, and with a bit of luck he may give us a few pointers.'

Eyeing Sheila and Brenda in the window, she pushed on into the hotel, where the reception was unmanned, and turned into the bar.

Busy making coffee for guests, Freddie greeted her with a broad smile. 'Chief Inspector Feeney. Not often we have the pleasure of your company. Slumming are you? Or working on the side for the hotel inspectors?'

She scowled. 'Neither. I'm here to speak to one of your guests. Joe Murray.'

Freddie poured coffee for his customers and nodded to the window table. 'His friends are there. I believe he's thawing out in the bath.' Placing the cups on saucers, he asked, 'Is it about Ginny Nicholson?'

'It is, and don't you go too far. I'll be speaking to you about her before the day is out.'

If Freddie was worried, his smile belied it. 'Poor Ginny. Fancy someone bumping off a poor, defenceless woman like that.'

'And where were you between nine and nine thirty this morning, Delaney?' Holmes demanded.

Freddie's good cheer was not disrupted. 'Right here, Mr 'Olmes.' He deliberately mimicked Dennis Hoey who had played Inspector Lestrade opposite Basil Rathbone's Sherlock

Holmes in a number of films. 'And my missus and my staff, *and* a number of guests will verify that.'

'And of course, you wouldn't be seen with her, would you?' the sergeant pressed.

'Now why would a successful businessman like me break the rules, Sergeant?' Freddie's smile faded. 'I have had no contact with her, and I had no reason to kill her. All right?'

'We're told she was drinking in here last night.'

Freddie grinned. 'Was she? Well, we're pretty full, you know. I can't say I noticed her.'

'We'll be talking more seriously later, Mr Delaney.' Feeney turned away, crossed the room and stood, towering above Sheila and Brenda. 'Mrs Riley, Mrs Jump. I came to speak to Mr Murray. Is he not here?'

Both women put down their work on the bonnets.

'He'll be down shortly,' Sheila assured her. 'Can we help?'

'Possibly.' Feeney nodded to the chair opposite Sheila. 'May I?' She sat down, Holmes claimed the empty chair alongside her, and took out his pocketbook. 'Preparing for the Easter Bonnet Parade?'

'It's for charity, and it gives us something to occupy our minds until the rain stops. We're very big on charity oop north.' Brenda deliberately exaggerated her accent.

'Highly commendable.'

Sheila played with her cup and saucer. 'I'm sure you didn't come here to talk about the Easter bonnet competition, Chief Inspector.'

'You're correct, Mrs Riley, which is why I asked about Mr Murray. However, you were on Regent Street yesterday when Mr Murray had the, er, spat with Ms Nicholson, weren't you?'

'Yes,' Brenda replied for both of them. 'But it was nothing. Not even a spat. The woman was arguing with the redhead Joe told you about. She threw the egg at the redhead, but Joe happened to get in the way. The redhead wandered off, and Joe and Ms Nicholson settled the matter quite amicably. And we've told you once, Joe was with one or other or both of us all morning. He did not kill the woman.'

'I don't say he did,' Feeney admitted. 'What I want to know is whether you – or he – took particular notice of this redhead.'

'We think it was the same woman who got into an argument with our bus driver as we came into Weston yesterday,' Sheila replied. 'At least, that's what Joe believes.'

'You think she may have killed Ginny?' Brenda asked.

'We're keeping an open mind, Mrs Jump. There are some background issues we have to consider while we're looking for suspects, and yesterday's, tête-à-tête may have some bearing on her death. Right now, we're simply keen to talk to this red-haired woman.' Feeney shifted the emphasis slightly. 'Your Mr Murray is quite well known for his deductive skills, isn't he?'

Brenda laughed. 'He's better known for his moods. As grumpy old men go, Joe takes the Blue

Riband. But he's sharp-eyed and more than capable of stringing an argument together based on his observations.'

'Even if most of those arguments are wrong,' Sheila added with a smile.

'My worry, Mrs Riley, is that he may find himself out of his depth. I said there are background issues, which I won't go into, but anyone who, er, pokes their nose in, to quote Mr Murray, may find it forcibly pushed out again.'

'It won't stop Joe,' Brenda declared. 'He's been threatened before.'

'He's even been threatened in the café, but he has Lee to back him up there.'

'His nephew,' Brenda explained. 'A former rugby player. Built a bit like yon fella.' She gestured at Freddie. 'You'll find, Chief Inspector, that Joe can't be frightened off... not even by you.'

* * *

Joe was not surprised to see Feeney and Holmes when he entered the bar.

Having warmed through in the bath, changed into a comfortable pair of denims and a clean shirt, he had bagged up his wet clothing for laundering, donned his ubiquitous gilet and picking up his topcoat, made his way down to the bar where he called for a cup of tea before joining his companions by the window.

'Change your mind, Chief Inspector?' he asked, taking out his tobacco tin and rolling a cigarette. 'You need my help?'

'I need information, Mr Murray, and you may have it.' Feeney repeated the question she had put to the two women.

Joe's face went blank, his mind's eye tracking back over the incident of the previous day, visualising every second of it, and what had been going on around it.

'I was making for the pub and Ginny was giving the redhead a real mouthful. The redhead wasn't impressed.'

'Would you recognise the redhead again if you saw her?' Feeney asked as Holmes made notes.

'Both times we saw her, she was carrying this bloody great handbag and a large Easter egg.' Freddie stood by the table with Joe's tea. Joe took it, and shook his head at the police. 'I don't think I've seen her face. I mean, if she was carrying the handbag and egg and wearing the same clothing, sure, but otherwise…' He stirred milk and sugar into his tea and sipped approvingly. 'You think she may have killed Ginny because of the argument?'

'As I said to your friends, there are background issues which I won't go into, and it's possible that the redhead was involved. You didn't hear what the argument was about?'

'No.' Joe took out his cigarette rolling material. 'And Ginny wasn't forthcoming on it either.' He quickly rolled the cigarette and tucked it in his shirt pocket. 'So what are these background issues?'

'A matter for us, Mr Murray,' Feeney insisted.

Joe drank more tea. 'I've met your kind of chief inspector before, you know. Determined that it's your case, and perfectly happy to follow all the blind alleys until you find the through route, instead of asking for help when it's offered. I'm not about to steal your thunder, you know. I never do.'

Feeney glanced over her shoulder at the bar where Freddie and Hazel were deep in discussion. Turning back to face Joe, she murmured, 'Not here.'

Joe stood up. 'Good. I need a smoke anyway.' He put on his fleece. 'Let's step outside.' Making for the door, he called out, 'Hey, Freddie, don't take my cup and saucer. I'm just nipping out for a smoke.'

'No problem, Joe,' Freddie assured him. 'Can't say I like your choice of company, though.'

'Us poor Yorkshire folk are beggars, my friend, so we can't be choosers.'

Stepping out into the rain, Joe found a table where the seats, sheltering under the parasol, were comparatively dry, sat down, and cupping his hands around his Zippo, lit his cigarette. He drew the smoke deep into his lungs and let it out with satisfied hiss.

'For a poor Yorkshireman, you appear to enjoy the finer things in life, Mr Murray,' Feeney said. 'That cigarette lighter must have cost a small fortune.'

'A fiftieth birthday present from my two best friends, Sheila and Brenda, who, coincidentally, are also two of my staff.'

'You make an above average income from your café?' the chief inspector persisted.

'What is this? Are you moonlighting as a VAT inspector? I make a good living. Not grand, but adequate.'

'And what do you drive? Mercedes? Jaguar?'

Blowing out a cloud of smoke, watching it whipped away by the wind, Joe tutted. 'A beat up old Vauxhall. Is this relevant?'

Feeney did not answer immediately. Instead, she reached into her briefcase, drew out a photograph, and handed it to Joe. 'Is this the woman you saw?'

Joe studied the large print. A bus in the background told him the picture had been taken in London. The woman was walking along the street towards the cameraman, a large handbag hooked over her left arm. Her face was narrow and pinched, the eyes set close together, the mouth small and turned down in a grimace. Her red hair looked as if it was pulled into a ponytail. The weather was better when the picture was taken. She wore no coat, only a striped sweater and a pair of old, shabby jogging pants.

'The hair colour is right, so it could be. The handbag is certainly large enough and it looks like the woman I saw yesterday, but as I've already told you, I've never seen her face, so I couldn't be certain.' Joe handed the photograph back. 'Who is she?'

'Her name is Diane Shipton, and if she's in Weston-super-Mare, I want to know about it.'

'She's a killer?'

'She has never been known to commit any sort of violent act, but her husband, Gil, has served time for assault.' Feeney put the photograph back in its folder. 'Let me tell you something about her and Gil. She used to be a reporter with a London daily. Then she became a dirt-digger for a Sunday tabloid, and finally, about ten years ago, she went freelance. According to HMRC, She makes a moderate income, and yet Gil, who doesn't work at all, drives a nearly new BMW.'

Joe shrugged. 'They were obviously careful with money when she worked for the press.'

Holmes smiled. 'The Beamer was a gift from a grateful client. Diane was the ghost writer for his biography. The book did well, so in addition to her fees, he gave her the Beamer.'

'It all sounds reasonable to me,' Joe said.

'The Metropolitan Police have a different theory,' Holmes said.

Chief Inspector Feeney took up the tale. 'The gentleman who gave the Shiptons the BMW was a former surgeon. Highly respected in his day, but he retired under something of a cloud. There were unproven allegations of drunkenness made against him. It was all very hush-hush. The Met believe that there was some substance to the allegations, even though the good doctor still denies them. They also believe that Diane Shipton got hold of proof and blackmailed him. And *that* is why he gave her the car.'

Joe whistled and relit his cigarette. 'So you're never going to prove it without his testimony, and he won't testify because it would expose the truth about his drinking.'

'Correct,' Feeney agreed. 'London believe that Diane is making use of her dirt-digging skills to supplement her income by blackmailing any number of people. But of course, there is not one scrap of evidence. Surveillance has proved costly and pointless. Whenever the Met have spoken to people she's seen meeting, they've drawn a blank. She's an old friend, she's an old colleague, an old girlfriend.'

'And until the day someone finds enough bottle to talk, you'll never get her.'

'Again correct.'

Joe puffed on his cigarette, his eyes distant, as if he were studying the rain pouring on the Grand Pier, his lively mind sorting and sifting all he had just learned. 'Where does this all fit in with Virginia Nicholson's murder? Are you saying Diane Shipton had something on Ginny?'

'If Diane Shipton is here in Weston, and if she was involved in yesterday's argument, then it's possible.' Feeney hesitated a moment. 'I'm going to tell you something that is not generally known, Mr Murray. Virginia was a pillar of this community. She was well-liked, a tireless charity worker, and she was even a councillor for a short while. Independent; not aligned with any political party.' Again the chief inspector paused. 'She was also a convicted killer, serving a life sentence, and released only on licence.'

Taking a drag from his cigarette while Feeney spoke, Joe almost choked on the tobacco. 'What?'

'In the early nineties, she was raped – so she

claimed. Instead of reporting the matter to the police, which she claimed would have been pointless, she went after her attacker and stabbed him to death, then handed herself in.'

'Sounds to me like he got what he deserved,' Joe said.

'Most people would agree, Mr Murray, and had she reported the matter to us first, then gone after him, the courts might have looked upon her crime more leniently. As it was, her plea in mitigation was not accepted, she was found guilty and sentenced to life imprisonment. That was in 1992. She was released on licence eight years later, and moved here, to Weston-super-Mare, to start a new life. Naturally, we were aware of the situation. All life-prisoners, when released on licence, must report to the local police when they move. However, we were the only ones who knew of her past, and I can guarantee the confidentiality of that information. Weston is a friendly town, but Virginia Nicholson would not have lasted long here if people had learned of her past.'

Joe nodded and pulled on the cigarette again. It had gone out. Digging out his Zippo, he relit it, his furrowed brow creasing further. 'I can see where you're going with all this, but you can't do anything until and unless you can demonstrate that not only is this Shipton woman here in Weston, but that it was her Ginny argued with and she was in the vicinity at the time of Ginny's murder. Any news from Clifftop Park?'

'You were right about the Easter eggs,' Feeney replied. 'We've accounted for a hundred and ninety-two, and we didn't count yours or your friends.'

'Another five, I think,' Joe said.

'In that case, we're close enough to the total to conclude that Virginia was either finished or almost finished when she was intercepted and murdered. We've found the carrier bags in which she had the eggs, and we've found her handbag. Purse is missing, obviously.'

Joe nodded. 'That would help make it look like a robbery?'

'It may actually be a robbery,' Sergeant Holmes pointed out, and Feeney backed him up.

'You, yourself pointed out, Joe, that there were always two possibilities for this crime. Planned and opportunist. If it was opportunist, then the motive is likely to be robbery.'

Taking a final pull on his cigarette, Joe crushed it out. 'So what's the point of telling me all this? Are you asking for my help or trying to warn me off?'

It appeared to him that Feeney was choosing her words carefully. 'We don't really need your help, Mr Murray. And I certainly wouldn't warn you off, because according to the best of my information, you'd only ignore me. But if this really is Diane Shipton at work, then she is a very dangerous lady, and if you begin asking the wrong questions of her, you could end up hurt or worse.'

Joe stood up. 'Right. Point taken. If I see her, I'll keep my distance and bell you instead of shoving my oar in. That good enough for you?'

'Perfect,' Feeney agreed. 'But there's

something else I'd like to ask of you.' In the act of rising, Joe paused and sat down again. 'You're here on holiday and like all holidaymakers, you have a camera. Yes?'

He nodded. 'As it happens, I have two... three if you count the one on my smartphone.'

'Good. If you see this redhead, could you take a sneaky picture of her? Try not to make it obvious, but get us some kind of image we can study.'

Joe stood again. 'Yeah, no problem.' There was a long moment of silence. Joe took it as a cue. 'Well, if that's it, I'm going back inside to finish my tea.'

'And we'll take our leave of you. Thank you for your help.'

Joe ambled back into the hotel and rejoined the women.

'Any the wiser?' Brenda asked, as she sewed a small, fluffy lamb onto the brim of her bonnet.

'A bit, and I think Feeney has it right. I should mind my own business. It's not my usual line of investigation.'

Sheila held her bonnet in front of her so she could judge the effect of yellow paper roses glued to the brim. 'Now there's a novelty. Joe Murray admitting he may be out of his depth.'

'I may be stupid enough to employ you two, but I'm not totally suicidal.' Joe cast a sour eye over their handiwork. 'Listen, all this faffing about with hats, how much is the first prize again?'

'A voucher for twenty pounds,' Brenda said without taking her eyes off her sewing, 'which you can spend in any number of shops in the town.'

'So let me work this out. The hats and the bits and pieces cost you about a fiver. The entry fee was a tenner. So if you win, you'll come away with a profit of five pounds, but it can only be spent here in Weston-super-Mare.'

Sheila put down her hat. 'It's not about profit, Joe, it's for charity. Now if you've nothing better to do than criticise, take yourself to the bar and get fresh coffee.'

'And cakes,' Brenda added.

Joe drank his rapidly cooling tea, collected all the cups and made his way to the bar. 'Fill 'em up again, please, Freddie. Two coffees, one tea, and do you have any cakes?'

'Sorry, Joe, but we're a hotel, not a tea room. All we have is what you see.' Taking the cups and getting out fresh ones, Freddie gestured at the glass display case, where he stored potato crisps, packets of peanuts and small packets of biscuits.

'I'll take two packets of those oatmeal biscuits, too,' Joe ordered and dug out his wallet.

'Old Bill done with you, have they?' Freddie asked as the coffee dispenser frothed.

'Routine stuff. The woman who was murdered up in Clifftop Park. She was a lifer.'

'Tell us something we don't know, mate.' Freddie replied and filled two cups with coffee. 'Not general knowledge round Weston, but there were a few of us in the know.' He filled a small, metal teapot, and set everything on a tray for Joe. 'Killed some bloke who insisted on having his wicked way with her after she said no... or so she claimed.'

'What? You don't believe it?'

Freddie placed the drinks on a tray and grinned at Joe. 'Not up to me to believe or disbelieve, matey. It's all about whether the family of the bloke she killed found her and decided to extract a bit of street justice. That's three pounds eighty for cash, Joe.'

Joe handed over a fiver. 'I never thought of that. You reckon that's what may have happened? Only the law are thinking on some woman called Diane Shipton.'

Freddie rang up the sale, and handed over change. With a forced, humorous gleam in his eye, he said, 'Take it from someone who knows. Diane Shipton may be a blackmailer, but she's no killer.'

Chapter Five

The time was approaching one in the afternoon when Sheila and Brenda made their way first to their room on the floor below Joe's, to abandon their makeshift millinery, and then head for the town.

'I don't like this,' Brenda said as Sheila unlocked the door and led the way into the room. 'If we believe everything the police say, Joe could be running into trouble just taking a picture of the woman.'

'An undue level of concern, dear?' There was a twinkle of laughter in Sheila's voice, matched by a gleam in her eye.

Brenda returned a withering stare. 'Nothing of the kind. I don't think any more nor less of his lordship now than I ever did. I'd feel the same if it was George or Alec or, heaven forbid, Les Tanner.' She placed her half-finished bonnet on the dresser next to Sheila's and reached into the wardrobe for her quilted anorak. Struggling into its close-fitting confines, she went on, 'We've known Joe all our lives, Sheila. When did he ever get into a fight and win?'

Pulling on her wax jacket, Sheila paused a moment to consider the question. 'Never. Not that I can recall, anyway.'

'Correct. Even when he got into a fight with Jean Woolmer, he lost, and she was a seven-year old schoolgirl.'

'Yes, but be fair, Brenda. Joe was only six, and Jean was tougher than most of the boys at school.'

'Even so, Joe is not a scrapper. He never has been. I'm not saying he's a coward; far from it. But he couldn't fight his way out of Mothercare in the New Year sales.' Brenda zipped up the anorak and picked up her handbag. 'The way the police describe them, these people sound more like gangsters than Lazy Luncheonette punters. Joe will need some kind of protection.'

Sheila smiled brightly. 'He has us.'

'I was thinking of someone a bit tougher. George, for instance. And his mate, Owen Frickley. They can go some.'

With her coat zipped and buttoned, Sheila made for the door. 'And you know about that, Brenda. But like the rest of us, they're here for a rest. Can you persuade them to become Joe's minders?'

Brenda locked the door behind them and grinned savagely. 'You leave George Robson to me. By the time I've done with him, he'll be ready to stand guard on the Prime Minister… and you know how much George hates politicians.'

* * *

Driven by fierce gales, the rain continued to hammer at the seafront, and when they left the Leeward, Joe and his companions could see the crowds sheltering on the covered pier. Umbrellas were out of the question, and by the time they had covered the five hundred yards from the hotel to the Winter Gardens, they were soaked.

Built in the 1920s, with an air of art deco about the alabaster columns and high windows, the deserted outdoor seating areas of the bar and the coffee shop appeared forgotten and forlorn in the foul weather, while through the high windows, they could see the interior seating areas were crowded. As they approached the classical grandeur of the main pavilion entrance, they could see a steady stream of people making their way in, and as many coming out.

'Something going on here,' Joe observed. 'Let's duck in and dry off for a few minutes.'

'Yes, boss,' Brenda agreed and, tapping at her mobile phone, followed her two friends into the building.

Once inside, the flow of people in both directions was centred on the Prince Consort Room, second largest of the conference/banqueting facilities. To their surprise, the event was not an event at all. Instead people were queuing to place Easter eggs, Easter bunnies and other assorted holiday items on a row of trestle tables to one side of the grand ballroom.

'What are they doing?' Joe asked. 'Trying for the world record in Easter egg pyramids?'

'What are you like?' Brenda gave him a playful shove in the back. 'You know full well what they're doing. Freddie told you. They're donating items for charity.'

'Charity? Again? Is this town the most charitable in England, or what?'

'Most towns are the same, Joe. It's just that you're so wrapped up in business you don't notice.'

'So what are they gonna do with them all?' Joe asked

'Distribute them to orphanages and hospitals, I believe.' Sheila frowned at Brenda. 'We should have bought Easter eggs or souvenirs. Something we could have added to the stand.'

Brenda volunteered. 'Tell you what. Why don't you and the master wait here while I'll nip round the corner, buy three eggs and we can add them?'

'Sounds good,' Sheila agreed. 'Would you like me to come with you?'

'No, no. No sense all of us getting wet.' Brenda zipped up her coat again. 'Five pounds each?' When Sheila nodded, she checked with Joe. 'All right?'

He fished out his wallet. 'So long as it's no more than a fiver. Need the money?'

'We can sort it out when I get back.'

Joe nodded. 'We'll wait in the café for you.'

Brenda made her way back out into the rain, Joe and Sheila moved through to the Prom Café, where he queued for tea and Sheila secured them a table by the window.

The place was busy; busier than usual thanks largely to the rain Joe guessed as he shuffled his way along the line at the service counter. It was a full ten minutes by the time he joined Sheila. Settling into his seat, casting a glance around the café, and seeing only people like themselves (wet, and glad of the shelter and a warming drink) he, instead, gazed through the windows towards the pier.

'What is it about the seaside that we all find so relaxing?' he asked.

'A question that's troubled psychologists for a century or more, Joe. I suppose the sea stands for freedom from the drudgery of work. At least, to us townies it might. If you're fisherman, I don't think you'd view it with quiet the same sense of calm.' Sheila sipped delicately at her tea. 'A more important question is, are you mellowing?'

The question puzzled Joe. 'I don't think so.'

'You barely raised a word of protest when Brenda suggested five pounds each on Easter eggs for charity.' A secretive smile crept across Sheila's lips. 'Or is it your new-found, deeper familiarity with Brenda having its effect?'

Joe reflected the smile, but his was more cynical. 'Ah. Right. Brenda's told you, has she? When we were on that stupid egg hunt this morning, she told me she hadn't.'

'She told me about it while you were upstairs getting changed. You don't think she should have done?'

Joe sipped his coffee and mentally rehearsed his answer. 'What I think, Sheila, is that it's none of your business.' He held up his hand as Sheila opened her mouth to interrupt. 'Let me finish. We're old friends. The three of us. We go all the way back to primary school. After Lee and Cheryl, you and Brenda are the closest thing I have to family. I really don't believe it's any of your business, but I don't think Brenda did wrong by telling you. There is the chance that it might have an effect on our friendship and working relationship.'

Sheila gave him a mock round of applause. 'Well done, Joe. I didn't think you had such consideration in you. You're not the most sensitive or diplomatic of men.'

She, too, allowed a moment of silence, and Joe, guessing she was choosing her next words carefully, steeled himself for some frank opinions. There had been many arguments between the three over the years, even in the days before the two women came to work for him, but although he probably came top for inadvertently piercing the skin, Sheila and Brenda were perfectly capable of getting to him.

'My concern, Joe, is not what you and Brenda get up to. That is, as you say, your affair – no pun intended – and I know it's been going on for some time. I'm not bothered for myself, either. I'm more worried about the effect on you two. Getting more deeply involved can put a strain on easy going relationships, and I wouldn't want to work in an atmosphere of mutual animosity between the two of you. Worse than that, I don't want to play go-between if and when things, er, go wrong. If you seriously think I'm poking my nose in, then please say so, but I really am worried about you two.'

'You think I didn't think about that? You think Brenda didn't think about it? It wasn't intentional, Sheila. It's just, sort of happened, sine Valentine.'

He sighed and gazed through the windows once more. An open top bus passed by, heading north, towards their hotel. The lower deck appeared full, but there was no one seated upstairs. Why would there be in this foul weather?

The incessant rain and blustery winds perfectly matched his turgid feelings. The question of Brenda had been on his mind, too, ever since that morning in February when they had woken up together, their memories of the previous night no more than hazy, ill-defined mental images.

Joe and Brenda had dated for a short while in their teens. His father's demands upon his time (even then he had to be up at five thirty to help out in the café) had soon put paid to any potential relationship, and throughout his life, Joe had often wondered what would have become of them if it had not been for his responsibilities. Now, with one broken marriage – again thanks to the café – behind him, he wasn't altogether sure he wanted an answer.

Bringing his attention back to Sheila, he said, 'I don't think it's anything more than we want it to be. Sex.' He felt his ears colouring as he said the word. 'I'm not sure I want it to be anything more than that, and I don't think Brenda wants it to be any more than that, it's just that it's happening mor e often.' He sighed again. 'You know what Brenda's like.'

'Ever since Colin died, she's done her best to enjoy herself.' Sheila's lips tightened. 'I don't always approve, but it's her life to lead as she sees fit. She misses Colin, but I think his death brought home to her just how short life is. Peter's death came as a shock to me. Even after the first heart attack, I thought he was on the mend. Colin's was not a shock.'

'I remember. He was diagnosed a year before he died, wasn't he?'

Sheila nodded. 'A terrible, wasting disease. Her, er… oh, I don't know. Her ways with men are, I think, a reaction to the way Colin died, and, of course, the way she was widowed so young. She knows that what happened to Colin can happen to any of us. He didn't smoke, you know, and he drank only in moderation. He was fit and healthy, too. He looked after himself, and yet, the cancer still got to him. That must have had an effect on Brenda's mindset. So she enjoys herself with an attitude that's often mistaken for promiscuity.' Sheila narrowed her eyes on Joe. 'She dates a number of men, but she doesn't sleep with them all.'

'I know.' Joe took out his tobacco, his natural reaction to deeper debates. 'If you're worried that Brenda is simply freewheeling and I may be taking it more seriously, don't.' He ran a fine line of tobacco along the V of the cigarette paper. 'I had that Valentine's date with Letty, if you remember. I liked her. She could maybe have become Mrs Joe Murray, mark two, but I remember saying to her that it would take a long time for me to come to such a decision.'

'And Alison?' Sheila asked.

Licking the gummed edge of the paper, he completed the cigarette and dropped it into his shirt pocket for later consumption. 'Yes. Alison. I loved her, you know... well, as close as I could come to loving anyone, but it all went wrong because of the Lazy Luncheonette. Living and working together just didn't pan out. My old dad had the right answer. Ma never worked in the café. I did, so did our Arthur, before he cleared off to Oz, but my old queen stayed upstairs and kept house. She and Dad saw nothing of one another during the day. Maybe if I'd insisted Alison take a back seat, we could have survived, but...' He sighed again. 'I got it wrong, Sheila. I thought it would save on the wage bill if Alison worked with me. It did, but it wrecked our life together.' A semi-humorous gleam came into his eye. 'I'm not about to rush into the same mistake again. For the time being, we might be seeing more of each other, but I'll still treat my time with Brenda the way she does. A bit of fun when we feel like it. Nothing more.'

Sheila, too, injected some humour into her voice. 'I'm glad. I'll be watching you both, so be good.'

'Well, if I can't be good, I'll be careful.' Joe turned to gaze through the windows again. 'Hey, is that a bit of sunshine over there.' He pointed to the southwest where in the far distance, a tiny, golden break showed in the leaden sky.

'Better weather coming our way, I hope.'

'Not all that's coming our way, either.' Joe's gaze had come nearer to them, and a woman hurrying along the pavements, a large Easter egg clutched under her arm, the hood of her white anorak hiding her red hair.

He reached into his cagoule for his compact camera.

'Oh, right. That was quick.'

Sheila's comment puzzled Joe, but when he looked behind Diane Shipton, he saw Brenda hurrying along, a carrier bag in one hand, through which bulged the angular boxes of Easter eggs, her mobile phone in the other hand, tucked inside her hood while she spoke to someone. Some yards behind Brenda were two stocky men, and another redhead, ambling along in the same direction. A bell rang in Joe's head, but he ignored it. He had more important things to think about.

Gulping down his coffee, he urged, 'Let's get out and meet Brenda.'

'She'll be cold, Joe,' Sheila insisted. 'She'll want a cup of tea.'

'Yeah, well she can have one when we've handed over the Easter eggs. Come on, Sheila. Hurry up. I don't want to miss her.'

Hurrying after him as he made for the exit, Sheila remained puzzled. 'Miss Brenda? You can't miss Brenda. She has our eggs, too.'

Emerging into the entrance hall as Brenda came in, Joe looked around and caught sight of Diane Shipton's back disappearing into the Prince Consort Room.

'Ah. You're here. I could do with—'

'Quick, Brenda,' Joe interrupted. 'Our redhead is in there. Get one of the eggs, tag on behind her and I'll take a photograph.'

'Joe, I, er, who? What?'

Snatching the carrier from her, Joe removed one of the Easter eggs and handed it to Brenda. 'Just do it.'

'I need the ladies,' Brenda hissed quietly.

'After you've put the egg up. Come on.' He grabbed her by the hand and dragged her to the Prince Consort Room. 'Hurry up or you'll be too late.'

Brenda snatched her hand free. 'Joe. I need the toilet.'

'Tie a knot in it,' he insisted. 'Now will you hurry up?'

'I can't tie a knot in it. I'm not a man.'

'Stop bloody arguing.'

Brenda yielded and followed him, hurrying into the room and joining the short queue behind Diane Shipton. Joe stood back to one side and switched on his camera. He sensed Sheila at his shoulder.

Across the room Robert Quigley was still watching with approval, which suddenly turned to concern. Diane placed her giant Easter egg on the stand, stood back a moment to admire it, then turned to walk away. Shuffling uncomfortably, Brenda glanced back at Joe, who nodded and raised his camera to study the display.

Diane was perfectly framed in the shot and Brenda was right behind her, placing her Easter egg. Joe hit the button, the camera flashed and he took a moment to study the result. Perfect. Feeney would have no trouble identifying Diane.

Someone nudged his shoulder.

'What is it, Sheila? I'm busy.'

There was another nudge, harder this time, and a deliberately aimed hand dashed the camera from his grasp. The hand was backed up by a thick, sinewy and hairy wrist.

The camera dropped and skittered across the floor, where a heavy boot landed on it.

'Hey.'

'Oops. Sorry, pal.' The swarthy individual attached to the boot, bent down and collected the camera. 'Oh dear. Looks like it's broke. You should be more careful, mate.'

Joe turned to the man closer to him, another muscular individual, his clean shaven features split into a broad grin of pure menace. 'It'd be more to the point if you were careful about who you were taking pictures of.'

Joe felt his legs trembling and his anger rising. He pointed to Brenda. 'She's a friend. I was taking a picture of her.'

'I don't think I believe you. In fact, I think you were taking a picture of my missus.' The nearer man gestured at Diane, who stood some yards away with the other woman, who look so like Diane that Joe assumed to be sisters.

'You think?' Joe demanded, snatching the remains of his crushed camera. 'You have enough brain cells to be able to think?'

Shipton (that was Joe's assumption) snatched at Joe's cagoule. 'You—'

'Knock it off unless you fancy a proper ruck in here.'

At the sound of George Robson's voice, Joe breathed a sigh of relief. He half turned his head to find George, Owen Frickley, Alec Staines and Mort Norris stood in a line, behind the two women.

The two men eyed Joe's friends, then each other. Across the hall, Quigley watched the proceedings with a worried eye as he spoke into his mobile phone.

Chewing spit, Shipton released Joe. 'Just watch your step, pal. You could get hurt.' He turned and marched off, snapping his fingers to the other three, who fell obediently in step behind him.

Joe breathed a sigh of relief at his fellow 3rd Age Club members. 'Thanks, guys. Thought I'd had it then. What are you doing here?'

'Brenda rang us,' George said. 'Warned us you might be in trouble. Didn't you, Bren... oh. She's gone.'

'She's in the ladies,' Sheila said. She swung a disapproving face on Joe. 'What on earth do you think you're playing at?'

'Feeney asked me if I could get a picture of our redhead; Diane Shipton.'

'I'm sure she didn't tell you to risk your stupid neck to do it.' Sheila waved a flailing hand at the busted camera. 'And look at the state of that. A complete waste of time and it's cost you your camera.'

'Doesn't make any difference.' Joe prised open the mangled back, and removed the memory card. He smiled broadly. 'I think I gave twenty quid for the camera, and it was crap, but the pictures are all stored on here. The minute Brenda comes back, I'm off to the cop shop with it.'

Chapter Six

The police station was housed in an ageing, four-storey, grey concrete block just off the main road to the motorway, and not far from the town centre. It reminded Joe of so many similar blocks he had seen built in the seventies, only to fall into disrepair when suitable tenants could not be found. Dour and forbidding. Sanford was full of such places; busy when the mine and the foundry were the heart of the town, empty eyesores now that the local economy had floundered.

Shown to Chief Inspector's Feeney's office, as cold, bare and as dour as the rest of the building, she arranged a cup of tea while they engaged in small talk.

'Our cop shop in Sanford is like this,' Joe told her. 'Only much older. Victorian, you know.'

'We're not long for this place, Mr Murray. I'm not even based here. I'm based in Bristol, and this station is soon to become an appointment only site. Major crime will be handled from Bristol and this will be the base for a few community constables, no more.'

Joe sympathised. 'Sign of the times.'

But if Feeney was convivial enough when it came to chatter, after handing the memory card to Sergeant Holmes, her annoyance rose when listening to Joe's account of events in the Winter Gardens.

'I did warn you how dangerous this woman

can be, Mr Murray. Not so much her, but her husband and brother-in-law.'

'I tried to make it look as if I was taking a picture of my friend. And enough with the Mr Murray business, eh? Everyone calls me by my given name; Joe.'

There was a knock on the door, and Sergeant Holmes entered, carrying the memory card and several freshly printed pictures. He handed them to Feeney. 'It's her, ma'am. No doubt about it.'

Feeney studied the prints. 'Then the people you met, Joe, were undoubtedly Gil Shipton and Terry Badger. It was probably Terry who trod on your camera, and I imagine his wife, Elaine, who's Diane's sister, will have been there somewhere. She's easily recognised. She looks like younger version of Diane. '

'She was with them,' Joe said.

Feeney placed her hand flat on the desk. 'In that case, Joe, I must insist that you keep your distance.' She went on to Holmes. 'Sergeant, put out a call to all units. Be on the lookout for the Shiptons and the Badgers. When they're seen, they're to be brought in for questioning on the murder of Virginia Nicholson. Officers are not to approach alone, but call for backup. Understood?'

'Yes, ma'am.' Holmes left the office.

When the door closed behind her sergeant, Feeney beamed a fond smile on Joe. 'You've done well, and I thank you, but you mustn't take risks, Joe. It's fortunate that your friends were there. The fact that you were in a public place wouldn't have prevented them from frogmarching you out and dealing with you elsewhere.'

He chuckled. 'Yeah, well, it wasn't entirely accidental. Brenda has been worried about me.'

'Wise lady. Your, er, girlfriend?'

'Hell, no…' Guilt ran through Joe. How could he be so dismissive of one of his best friends? 'Well, sort of. She works for me, as you know, but we have this sort of, er, relationship. Nothing special, just more than boss and employee.'

'Well, go back and join her and enjoy the rest of the weekend, Joe. You've done us a good turn, and we'll take it from here.'

'Just before I leave, one thing puzzles me,' Joe admitted. 'Why would Diane Shipton kill Ginny? I keep thinking back to what I heard in the street, yesterday. Word for word, Diane said, 'that's the trouble with people like you. You don't know when someone's trying to do you a favour'. How is blackmailing someone doing them a favour, and how is killing them doing them a favour? It doesn't make a lot of sense.'

'You're sure that's what you heard Diane say?'

'Verbatim,' Joe assured the chief inspector. 'Y'see, I can understand where Diane is coming from on the blackmail angle. She demands, let's say, a grand, and she's doing Ginny a favour by not broadcasting her past. But why kill her after she refused to pay?'

'A couple of points,' Feeney said. 'First, we don't know that Diane did kill Virginia. It just seems a little too coincidental, that's all. She met Virginia yesterday, and Virginia died today. It could be completely unconnected. Second, and probably more important, Diane Shipton has never resorted to violence as far as we know. That has always been the hallmark of her husband and brother-in-law, and even then, we've never been able to prove anything against them in connection with Diane's suspected activities. We can build good cases against all four, but we have no concrete evidence. Thinking on Virginia's murder, it may be that Gil Shipton or Terry Badger decided to act alone, without reference to Diane. Right now, we need to question them. No more.' She chewed her lip. 'It would help if we could place any of them in the vicinity of Clifftop Park this morning.'

'There's no CCTV up there?'

Feeney nodded. 'Some, but it covers the main car park and entrance by the pavilion. We're having the tapes studied and analysed as we speak. I'll know more later today.' She stood and shook hands. 'Thank you, Joe. I won't take up any more of your time. Enjoy the rest of your stay in Weston.'

He smiled. 'I'll try.'

* * *

The rain had eased slightly when Joe stepped out into the street. The brighter sky he had noticed from the Winter Gardens café, had made its way closer, and over to the west there was a definite hint of spring showing through the thinning layer of clouds.

Feeling pleased with his day's work, he took out his mobile phone and dialled Sheila. 'Where are you?' he asked.

'Marks and Spencer's. What about you?'

'Just come out of the cop shop and I'm on my way to that pub I was gonna visit yesterday,' he told her. 'The Sword & Shield, I think it's called. Near the turnip.'

'The carrot.'

'I knew it was something you serve with roast beef and Yorkshire pudding.'

'Although to be truly accurate it's called The Silica.'

'And I'll be there are plenty of silly cl—'

'Joe.' Sheila's voice had a warning edge to it.

'I was going to say silly clots, who paid for it. Meet me in the pub; we'll have a quick snifter before you carry on shopping.'

Joe cut the connection and began walking. Cutting across the A370, the main road to the promenade to his left, and the motorway to his right, following his street plan, he ambled along a narrower street with various business premises on either side, and emerged by the Odeon Cinema. Its cream, tiled frontage and tower provided a nostalgic reminder of similar picture houses in Sanford, Leeds and Wakefield from his younger years, but he doubted that their modern offerings, a couple of sci-fi blockbusters and a remake of a major action adventure from the 1980s, would compare with the magic of the movies he had seen in his teens.

Turning left, he found himself at the upper

end of Regent Street and he could see the needle-like spire of The Silica, two hundred yards away. Strolling on towards it, he glanced across the road at the sandy-coloured front of a pub named The Prince, where Diane and Gil Shipton were stepping in through the front door.

For as long as he could recall, he had been "poking his nose" into mysteries and crimes, mostly in the Sanford area, but lately, thanks to the 3rd Age Club outings, in other towns and counties, but he did not consider himself a private detective. More a talented amateur, with a keen eye, and sharp sense of logic. After the Sanford Valentine Strangler, this was the biggest case he had ever confronted, and he was strongly tempted to follow the pair into The Prince. The confrontation in the Winter Gardens weighed heavily upon him, however. He was not a fighter. He never had been. Sharp-tongued, quick witted, but never sharp-footed or quick-fisted. If the Shiptons spotted him, there would be no George Robson or Mort Norris to help him out of the difficulty.

'What would a *real* detective do, Joe?' he muttered to himself.

And he'd seen enough movies and TV shows to know the answer. A real detective would go into the pub, and secrete himself within earshot, but out of sight of the pair to listen in on their conversation.

Could he? He knew nothing about the pub. Was it one of those modern ones, where the tables were cut off in booths, or was it an old-fashioned, traditional pub? The exterior appearance suggested the latter.

A fresh resolve gripped him. It was a pub, wasn't it? Gil Shipton or no Gil Shipton, he was entitled to drink there.

He glanced at his dim reflection in the windows of a Chinese restaurant. The pale blue cagoule and flat cap would give him away immediately. The Shiptons would recognise him instantly from the Winter Gardens. And if he walked into the pub with the hood up, it would look even more suspicious.

Ignoring the rain, he took off the cagoule and turned it inside out. It wasn't really reversible, but by tucking the pockets inside out, he could get away with it. Recalling a newsagents and souvenir shop a few yards back, he retraced his steps, walked in and a few minutes later came out with a copy of *The Times* and a plant pot style sun hat in white bearing the legend, *I ♥ Zummerzet*. He turned it inside out so it hid the badge, dropped it on his head, and tucked his flat cap in what was now his inner pocket.

Crossing the road to The Prince, he purposely avoided the same entrance the Shiptons had used, preferring a door a few yards further down the street. He found his legs trembling as he stepped into the bar, and forcibly reminded himself that he was entitled to be there.

The place was busy. Men and women stood around the bar as most of the tables were taken. Joe's active imagination painted a mental image of the place as it would have been in days gone by: lively, noisy, its patrons' business conducted under a fuggy pall of tobacco smoke, augmented perhaps, by music from a juke box.

A quick glance around told him that the Shiptons had chosen a table close to the door through which they had entered, and were deep in earnest conversation. Another table nearby had only one occupant, an elderly man studying form in the back pages of *The Racing Post*.

Securing a half of bitter, he made his way to the table and, standing with his back to the Shiptons, raised a permission-seeking eyebrow at the old man, who nodded.

'Sit y'down, m'dear.'

Joe sat and opened up his copy of *The Times*, burying his attention in its broadsheet pages. Behind him he sensed a pause in the conversation, as if both eyes were upon him.

Years of working in the noisy environment of the Lazy Luncheonette, where the chatter of drivers clashed with the clatter of pots and pans in the kitchens, should, in theory, have had a detrimental effect on his hearing, but in fact, it had done just the opposite. It had enabled him to edit out background noise to concentrate on the orders placed at the counter. Now he could easily cut out the sounds of a busy pub and the mutterings of the old boy opposite, who was trying to decide whether to lose his money in the 3.30 at Newcastle or the 4.15 at Kempton Park, and hone in on the Shiptons' conversation.

Diane was doing most of the talking, her voice not much more than an angry hiss.

'It's right out there, where you can't get at it,

Gil. And by tomorrow it'll be gone to god knows where. I'm the only one who can ever get it back.' There was a significant pause before Diane spoke again. 'You end it. Now. The pair of you. Either that or you take the risk of some kid handing it in and blowing the entire thing wide open.'

'No way would you do that,' Gil said. 'You'd go down, too.'

Diane laughed. 'With your record for the hard act? All I gotta do is tell 'em you threatened me, forced me into it. Sure I'll get probation or something, but you're the one who'll go down. You and her, and him.' There was another pause, then the sound of Diane slamming her glass on the table. 'It's make your mind up time, Gil. And you got less than twenty-four hours to sort it.'

Gil huffed out his breath, but there was no trace of frustration when he spoke. Instead, his rough, London accent remained calm and calculating.

'Diane, you're trying to hang onto something that ain't worth hanging onto. We're through. We've been done for a long time. Long before her.'

Joe's active and agile mind began to slot the information into different compartments, attempting to relate it to the murder of Ginny Nicholson. What he was hearing did not make complete sense, and Diane's next remark did little to help.

'It's nothing to do with us being through. It's her. I don't care what you do, and I don't care who you do it with, but not her. Put an end to it, or I'll put an end to everything else.'

Frowning irritably at the old chap's mutterings on a horse at Uttoxeter, Joe listened to Gil's next words and reflected that if they had been said to him, he would have been chilled to the bone.

'You're threatening me, Diane, and you know what happens to people who threaten me.'

Diane did not react and Gil pressed on.

'The way it is, is the way it is, and all your antics ain't gonna change that. Now why don't you grow up and accept it? We can still do business.'

'Our business is through.'

At that moment Joe's phone rang. Fishing into his pockets, he took it out, and keeping his voice low and gruff in an attempt to disguise it, said, 'Yes, Brenda?'

'Where the hell are you? We're in the Sword & Shield looking for you.'

Aware that silence had fallen behind him, and aware that he had made a mistake answering the call, Joe roughened his voice even further. 'I'm in another pub.'

'Oh. So much for your instructions, then, if you can't follow them yourself. You want us to meet you there, or are you coming here?'

'Gimme ten minutes.'

He shut the phone off to the accompaniment of a chair scraping backwards behind him. Putting the phone away, Joe, took an even closer interest in the newspaper, pressing his face so close to it that the print was almost a blur in front of his eyes.

He felt the slight movement of air as Diane hurried past him. He waited longer until he heard

Gil's chair pushed back and the big man move to the bar. Then he folded the newspaper, and without looking at the bar, stood up.

'Are you following us, or what?'

Gil Shipton's voice froze Joe. He slowly turned and looked up at the big man, not at the bar, but standing menacingly over him. Joe cleared his throat. 'I had to go looking for a new camera after you and your pal broke the other one. If I'd known you were here, I'd have looked somewhere else.'

'Looks like someone shoulda dressed you a bit better, too,' Gil observed. 'Now what business of yours is the business between me and my missus?'

'None,' Joe lied. 'I just like your company.'

Gil took a step forward. Joe held up a hand and shook his head. The head to head had developed some attention from those around them. 'I wouldn't do that, if I were you.' Joe aimed a finger at the bar. 'The landlord won't like it, my friends are waiting for me outside, and my solicitor is already in touch with the local police to see if they know anything about you.' Joe forced a smile. 'You'll be hearing from him.'

Gil sighed irritably. 'Get outta my face, pal. If I see you again, I might decide to rearrange yours.'

Joe shrugged, turned, and with a flush of relief, walked quickly out of the pub.

The Sword & Shield stood less than a hundred yards from The Prince, and Joe did not slacken his rushed pace. With occasional glances over his shoulder to ensure Gil was not following, he hurried along the busy pavements, weaving in and out of the crowds which appeared to be growing in the ever-decreasing rain.

He bumped into a large man. His heart leapt. He looked up into the grinning face of Freddie Delaney.

'Steady on, Joe. Damn near knocked me over.'

Joe breathed a sigh of relief. 'It's you. Thank God for that.'

'Who were you expecting? A terminator?'

'Not far off. I just had a head to head with Gil Shipton in that pub.' Joe waved back towards The Prince.

Freddie disapproved with a tut and a doleful shake of the head. 'You don't half pick some people to argue with, don't you? Take a tip, mate; stay clear of the Shiptons. They're trouble.'

'I'm okay now, Freddie. My friends are in the Sword & Shield.'

'All right, buddy. I got people to see. Look after yourself.'

With a nod, Joe hurried on to the Sword & Shield, burst into the pub, stared around, and spotted his two companions sat with George Robson and Owen Frickley under the windows.

Its location, closer to the seafront, probably accounted for the Sword & Shield's busier afternoon than that of The Prince. The bar was more crowded, the hum of conversation, orchestrated by the clink and clatter of glasses and the familiar chink of the cash register, filled the room more than it had done in The Prince. In the hearth a cheering, coal-effect fire glowed, the smell of pub grub filled the air, but it did nothing to allay Joe's anxiety. It would be too easy for a man, even one as big as Gil, to hide himself amongst the crowds, ready to pounce.

Only when he had insinuated himself between George and Brenda did Joe feel safe and begin to relax.

George was first to comment. 'Hey up, Joe, why are you reading *The Times*?'

'I wanted something a bit more upmarket to wrap your meat pies in when we get home.'

'Your coat's on inside out,' Owen observed.

George kept up the pressure. 'And where did you get that hat?'

'Take him to the lavatory,' Brenda insisted, 'and check his Y-fronts are not on back to front.'

Ignoring the ribald laughter, Joe dug out his wallet, and passed a twenty to Owen. 'Get a round of drinks in, while my blood pressure comes down.'

'Have you been arguing again?' Sheila asked. 'Someone upset you?'

'Not really. I bumped into the Shiptons again.'

'You mean that crowd from earlier?' George waited for Joe to nod. 'What? And they took you for a pint?'

Giving George a withering stare, Joe recounted only scant details, and when Owen returned from the crowded bar carrying a tray of ales and spirits, he told them the whole tale from start to finish. Typically, it was Sheila who reacted first when he had finished.

'Joe, stop playing the hero. How many times

has Chief Inspector Feeney asked you to keep out of it?'

'I just thought I might be able to help.'

'Sheila's right, buddy,' George said. 'Trying to help with people like these is the quickest way to take a long walk off the end of the pier at high tide with a couple of bricks tied round your feet. Leave it to the filth.'

'I know all that, but you know, it was worth it… I think.'

'He's playing detective again.' Brenda laughed. 'Hey up. It's not an "I love Zummerzet" hat he needs, it's his Sherlock deerstalker.'

'Bog off, you.' Joe sipped a half of bitter. 'What I overheard doesn't make sense. At least, it doesn't make complete sense.'

Several mouths opened to pass more comment, but Sheila hushed them all. 'What doesn't make sense, Joe?'

'Think about what Feeney told me. Diane is a blackmailer.'

'She also said they had no proof of that,' Brenda pointed out.

'This isn't a court of law, Brenda. We don't need proof and neither do the cops when they're pointing the finger. They need evidence, not proof.' Joe took out his tobacco and began to roll a cigarette, a process that helped clarify his thinking. 'So the plod assumed that Diane and the rest of her family are here putting the pressure on Ginny. But what I overheard was Diane grumbling about her husband's bit on the side, and threatening him with a stretch of porridge if he didn't pack it in.'

'You don't go to prison for adultery, do you?' Owen asked.

'Brenda had better hope not,' Joe replied, and the table dissolved into laughter.

The butt of this riposte took it in good part. 'If I'm going down, I'll be taking most of the married men in Sanford with me.'

'Get on with what you were saying, Joe,' Sheila insisted.

He completed his cigarette and dropped it in his shirt pocket. 'Right. So there's Diane threatening Gil with the chokey if he doesn't knock it off. He comes back at her saying she'd go down too, but she says, no. She won't. She'll get away with probation because of his record, by claiming he forced her to do it. Do what?'

'Kill Ginny?' Brenda suggested.

Joe shook his head and drank more lager. 'That's murder and that's what I mean about it not making complete sense. It's possible, I suppose, for someone to be coerced into killing, but even if it were proved, other than in rare circumstances, you wouldn't get off with probation. Sheila?'

Sheila drained off her first gin and tonic and, pushing the glass to the centre of the table, drew her second towards her. 'In very exceptional circumstances, you might get away with probation, but given the police's interest in Diane, I should think it highly unlikely. She would still go to prison, no matter how much she pleaded that her husband had forced her. But, Joe, her killing Virginia Nicholson doesn't square with the police account of the Shiptons' activities, anyway, does it?'

'No, it doesn't, but Diane's conversation does. She told Gil, and I quote, "It's right out there, where you can't get at it, Gil. And by tomorrow it'll be gone to god knows where." I don't know what "it"' is, but she also said she's the only one who'll be able to get it back. Now, if Gil can't follow it, whatever it is, how can Diane?'

George finished off his pint with a huge swallow. 'Tracking.'

'Huh?' Joe's comment was echoed by the puzzled gazes of the whole table.

'Tracking. Like satnav.' George repeated, placing his empty glass alongside Sheila's and picking up his fresh pint, drank from it. 'I have a mate who works for one of these parcel delivery firms in Leeds. Their customers can pay to have the parcels tracked. They have some kind of widget in the parcel, and the company can track it just like you do with a mobile phone. They know where it is at any time day or night. All they do is call up the wossname, parcel ID number, and it shows up on their computer.'

Joe, too, took a sip of his lager. 'George, that kind of setup would cost a fortune. Why would Diane go to all that trouble?'

'George has a point, Joe,' Sheila said. 'If she really is a blackmailer, Diane has probably made a lot of money over the years, and if this… whatever it is, contains incriminating information, which she would rather not let the police get hold of, it may be worth her while to have it tracked so she can retrieve it once her threat has produced results.

That is once her husband has agreed to end his affair with the other woman.'

Again Joe shook his head. 'That doesn't tally. Her precise words were, '"either that or you take the risk of some kid handing it in".' Joe put his glass down. 'Some kid. Not any specific kid, just some kid. It sounded to me like she didn't know where it would end up, either, but she had some means of finding out.'

'Obvious, then, innit?' Brenda said. 'It's the Easter egg she put on the stack in the Winter Gardens.'

All eyes turned upon her.

'Again?' Joe demanded.

'Where is all that chocolate and the rest of the goodies going? Orphanages, children's hospitals and such. Whatever it is, she's hidden it in that egg, and she has some method of finding out where it's going.'

Joe was still not satisfied. 'Such as?'

'The simplest method of all, I reckon.' Brenda swigged back her Campari. 'She'll ask. Isn't it you who keeps telling us most people are voice-operated, Joe? All you have to do is ask. All she'll do is ask the organiser where her egg went.'

Chapter Seven

'From a logistics point of view, it's quite an operation.' Robert Quigley's voice glowed with audible pride as he explained the process to Joe. 'I'm sure Weston-super-Mare is not the only town running this kind of event, but it's the only one in the Avon and Bristol area, and we've put an awful lot of work into the operation, all of which culminates on Sunday afternoon, after the Easter Bonnet Parade.'

Brenda's announcement in the Sword & Shield was so obvious that Joe felt irritated he had not thought of it first. But once she had spoken, he drained off his glass and insisted that they leave right away, and make their way to the Winter Gardens.

There was some delay while Brenda and Sheila finished their drinks. George and Owen complained that they had better things to do with their time than play nursemaid to Joe, and as a result, some minutes later, Joe and the two women stepped out of the pub into weak, watery sunshine, and pavements that were beginning to dry off.

'It's a pity they didn't leave the egg hunt until now,' Joe complained as he strode purposefully along the sidewalks.

'I'll bet Ginny Nicholson feels the same,' Brenda commented.

The improving weather had brought out many more people, emerging from the amusement arcades, shops and cafes to take in the fresh, warming, spring air. Joe found himself having to dodge and duck around crowds studying shop displays, or checking the menu boards outside the many eateries along Regent Street.

Their progress was also slowed by the two women's habit of pausing to look at clothes and shoes in every other shop, and Joe became increasingly frustrated at their occasional suggestions to, "hang on a minute," "look at that," or "you don't find them that cheap up our way."

It was just after four by the time they stepped into the Winter Gardens, and the Prince Consort Room, where Joe promptly badgered Quigley.

'After the Easter Bonnet Parade about four o'clock on Sunday, this will all be shipped into a large van and taken off to our distribution depot in Bristol.' Quigley gestured at the stack of chocolate and other gifts before him, and continued his lecture. 'From there, it will be put onto smaller vans, and by eight o'clock Sunday evening, they will be on their way to orphanages and children's hospitals and homes all over the Avon area. Those children will wake to a wonderful Easter surprise on Monday morning.'

'Isn't it a bit odd arranging everything for Monday?' Sheila asked. 'Wouldn't it have been better to have it all collected tomorrow so the children could have their gifts on Easter Day?'

Quigley sucked in his breath with the air of one about to exculpate himself from responsibility for something that had gone so obviously wrong. 'During the committee stage, it was felt that many of the children, particularly those in hospital, and to a lesser extent those in orphanages, would already receive treats on Easter Sunday, from parents or staff at the various institutes. Our efforts are aimed at giving them a little extra something on Monday.'

'What you mean is you couldn't get the hall for the Easter Bonnet thing until Sunday,' Joe said with a wave of the hand that took in the whole of the Prince Consort Room.

'Naturally, there were some difficulties with securing the venue, too. There's a Neil Diamond concert here tonight, and a gala Easter dinner and dance tomorrow night. Ours is a charity event, remember, and the Winter Gardens are run by a bona fide corporation, which needs to show a profit at the end of the financial year.' Quigley hurried on in an effort to gloss over the issue. 'In addition, we felt that holding the Easter Bonnet Parade on Sunday gave us an extra day for people, such as your good selves, to make their donations.' He smiled thinly. 'It also allowed visitors to the town, such as your good lady, more time to prepare their Easter bonnet.' On the words "your good lady", Quigley again gestured, a flaccid wave of the hand which could have indicated either Sheila or Brenda.

Joe hastened to correct him. 'My good lady buggered off to Tenerife years ago. These two are my stand-ins.'

Brenda smiled at Quigley. 'We make a good threesome.'

Nonplussed by the tongue in cheek responses,

Quigley again sucked in his breath. 'May I ask, did you have some concern over our arrangements, or are you simply interested in charity work?'

'I do my bit for charity by keeping these two in gainful employment. It saves them walking the streets.' Satisfied that he had once more ruffled Quigley's slightly snooty air, Joe went on, 'I put an egg on here earlier. Suppose I wanted to know who got that egg?'

'Impossible.' Quigley drew breath with an audible 'whoosh', preparing to deliver another lengthy lecture. 'None of the individual items is addressed, Mr Murray. When our large van gets to the depot, the gifts will be sorted according to category; Easter eggs, general sweets, soft toys, other toys, and so one, then broken down into further categories according to age ranges—'

'I didn't know Easter eggs had an age range,' Sheila interrupted.

Quigley delivered an owlish, niggled stare. 'I was thinking of the toys, madam.' Turning back to Joe, he pressed on. 'Once that categorisation is complete, the small vans will be loaded, taking one item at a time from each category by turn, so that when we're finished each of the vans will have a similar number of items from each category.'

'So if I wanted my Easter egg to go to, say, the children's ward at Sanford General Hospital, I couldn't do it?'

Quigley's malleable features fogged. 'I don't think I know Sanford General Hospital.'

'You wouldn't,' Joe assured him. 'It's in Sanford; where we come from.'

Quigley leapt upon the admission. 'But we're working specifically in the Avon and North Somerset area.'

Now Joe sighed, muttering, 'Give me strength,' under his breath. Aloud, he said, 'Just humour me for a minute, will you?' He moved closer to the stack and reached up to lay a hand on Diane Shipton's giant Easter egg, its smooth, gold foil perfectly marking out the hexagons of chocolate beneath. 'Suppose this was mine, and I wanted it delivered to a specific institution. You're telling me that I couldn't do that by leaving it with you?'

'No, sir, you could not. The only way you could ensure that would be by delivering it to the hospital, whether by parcel post or by hand, to the intended recipients.'

'Thank you.'

As he removed his hand Joe applied just enough pressure on the egg's outer case to topple it. It came crashing down, knocking over several soft toys and smaller Easter eggs, which scattered across the polished floor. Quigley appeared fit to have a heart attack, Brenda and Sheila both tutted loudly, and Joe promptly apologised.

'I am a clumsy bugger.'

He bent to begin picking up the loose items. Sheila and Brenda moved to help him. Sheila grabbed the giant egg he had deliberately dropped. Joe snatched it before her and there was a brief tug of war before a warning glance from Joe persuaded Sheila to let go. Meanwhile, Quigley flapped frantically around them.

With a practised eye, Joe examined the packaging around the egg. It appeared undisturbed. He pressed a finger gently against one corner of the gold foil, which also appeared undisturbed, and rather than the pliable feel of chocolate beneath, found it hard, unyielding.

Standing upright, he made to replace it on the stack, and surreptitiously rattled the box as he did so. Notwithstanding the outer packaging declaring the egg to be full of milk chocolates, there was, as far as he could judge, nothing inside.

He put the egg back on the display and turned to find Brenda holding two smaller eggs, both badly squashed.

'I am a berk,' he chortled and dug out his wallet. Taking out a five-pound note, he handed it to Quigley. 'Will a fiver cover it? With my apologies, of course.'

Quigley gazed snootily down his nose, but he took the money anyway and Joe and his two companions left the hall, making their way to the coffee room next door. As they left the Prince Consort Room Brenda began, 'What was that—' before Joe cut her off with a finger to his lips and a determined stare.

With the sun now shining, Joe secured a table outside, while Brenda and Sheila queued for food and drink.

The metal frames and polished, wooden seats of the chairs were still wet from the earlier rain. Joe spent a few minutes drying them off with paper napkins and his handkerchief before Sheila and Brenda joined him carrying trays of tea, coffee and cakes.

Helping himself to a cup of tea and an iced bun, Joe basked in the rising temperature and warm sunshine. Whenever he thought about the Sanford 3rd Age Club outings, this was the image he held in mind. Thanks to the vagaries of British weather, especially in recent years, it was rare that the image translated to reality, but when it did, he revelled in it.

'There may be something to be said for packing it all in and moving to the Costa Fortune, you know.'

Sorted with their coffee and cakes, Sheila and Brenda took a less philosophical view.

'Never mind Southern Spain. What was that little farce about, Joe?' Brenda asked.

In the face of her demands, he put on an unconvincing display of innocence. 'Farce?'

Sheila waded in on the attack. 'In all the years I've worked at the Lazy Luncheonette, I've never known you drop so much as a teaspoon, never mind knock down a display of Easter eggs and toys. In fact you spend most of your time telling Lee off for dropping plates.'

'Lee deserves it. He is a clumsy so-and-so. Always has been.'

'There you go again,' Brenda grumbled. 'Trying to sidetrack us. Forget Lee and tell us what you were doing in there.'

Joe grinned. 'Testing out our theory, and finding it wanting. There's something not right about the big Easter egg Diane placed on the stack. It doesn't feel right. To be honest, it feels more like a display model.'

The women exchanged glances. 'A what?' Brenda asked.

Joe bit off a mouthful of iced bun, chewed and swallowed it. 'They were quite the thing when I was a lad helping my old man in the café. You'd store your chocolate bars behind the counter, and the stuff out front, the display stock, might have looked like the real thing, but were actually wooden blocks supplied by the manufacturers, in the real wrappers.'

'And you think this is one?' Sheila demanded.

Joe shrugged, and finished off his bun. Taking out his tobacco tin, he said, 'All I'm saying is, it didn't feel like an Easter egg. Let's think what Diane may have hidden. Details of all their crimes, maybe? We said earlier that she wouldn't get away with murder, but she might sneak off on blackmail charges if she could persuade a jury that it was her husband who pressured her into doing it. Even if she did go to prison, as long as she could persuade the jury she was acting under duress, she might get a light sentence. Eighteen months, say, and with remission, she'd be out in nine months, while Gil goes down for at least ten, possibly longer if they can pin Ginny's murder on him.'

Brenda chewed on a cherry Bakewell, her brow knitted in thought. Alongside her, Sheila put down her Danish pastry, licked the cream from her fingers, took a sip of coffee, and said, 'That wouldn't get her husband back, though, would it?'

'The way I overheard the conversation, she doesn't want him back. It's not his malarkey she's complaining about. It's the woman he's fooling with.'

'And who's she?' Brenda asked through a mouthful of Bakewell tart.

'I don't know. They weren't using names. Probably worried about people earwigging.'

Brenda swallowed the cake. 'People like you, you mean?'

Joe chuckled and rolled a cigarette. Putting a light to it with his brass Zippo, he said, 'Let's get back to what I was saying. She has the information which can send them all down, and she's hidden it. Next thing I learn is she's put a display egg up on the stack here.' He waved up at the building behind them. 'What's the betting that the information is hidden in that fake egg?'

His rhetorical question was greeted with more, thoughtful silence.

Eventually, Sheila pouted eruditely. 'It makes sense I suppose.'

'Not very clever, though,' Brenda said. 'Putting it right there where anyone could get hold of it.'

'But it is clever,' Sheila said. 'We saw how protective Robert Quigley was about the gifts. It's right there, in full public view, and I'm willing to bet she is the only one who could go anywhere near it before it's shipped off to the sorting depot on Sunday.'

'Correct,' Joe said. He took a deep drag on his cigarette and blew the smoke out with a satisfied hiss. 'Except that it isn't.'

Sheila turned sharply on him and Brenda

laughed.

'What?'

'Come again?'

Joe took another drag on his cigarette. 'When I took the egg off you, Sheila, I checked it. I pressed the corners. That's how I knew it wasn't real. As I put it back up, I also shook it. You know how, if you shake a real Easter egg, you can feel the sweets inside moving around. Well I couldn't in this one. There's nothing in it.'

Sheila appeared furious, but Brenda saw the funny side of it.

'You never miss a trick, do you, Joe? Only this time you have.'

He took instant umbrage. 'What? How?'

'All that paper,' Brenda said. 'There must be pages of it, and if she jammed it in there properly, it wouldn't move around.'

Sheila expressed her satisfaction with the explanation. 'There you are. Simple.'

'Just like you two.' Joe ignored their irritation, sat forward and drank more tea. 'When are you going to come into the twenty-first century?' He reached into the pocket of his ubiquitous gilet, and came out with a memory stick. 'Eight gigabytes. It cost me a few quid in the local supermarket. You don't store documents on paper these days. You store them digitally on something like this. And if it's sensitive information, you use your nut and lock it up with a password. That wouldn't matter to Gil. He'd simply destroy it, but if the filth got hold of it, they'd have a hell of a time cracking the password.'

Sheila considered the information. 'It could still be in the fake egg, Joe. I'm assuming those things come apart?'

Joe shrugged and stubbed out his cigarette. 'I don't know. It's probably moulded plastic. Even if it doesn't come apart, it wouldn't take a genius to cut it in half to stash something inside. Why do you ask?'

'I'm thinking she may have packed it in cotton wool, or something. That way, if anyone did shake the egg, like you did, they'd detect nothing.'

Joe shook his head. 'You think that would stop Gil ripping the thing to pieces? No. I don't believe it. That egg is a fake, and it's been put there as a decoy. Gil is probably convinced that the information is in it, and he can't get at it. Meantime, she's stored the real thing somewhere else.'

'Where?' Brenda demanded.

'How the hell should I know? It could be at her place, at her bank, anywhere. All I'm sure of is that Gil will pull his hair out trying to get to it and if and when he does, he'll come up empty-handed.'

* * *

Running a brush through her dark hair, checking it in the dresser mirror, Brenda said, 'There's something nice as well as naughty about making love in the late afternoon.'

Perched on the edge of the freshly made bed, rolling a cigarette, Joe grunted. 'It may be the knowledge that you can go out and get plastered tonight without having to worry about your performance later.'

Brenda chuckled. 'It's you men who worry about performance. We women don't need to.' Her brown eyes gazed back at her through the mirror. The smile faded, and she turned to face him. 'Sheila knows. I told her this morning while you were taking a bath and thawing out.'

Still with his back to her, finishing off rolling his cigarette, Joe responded only slowly. 'Huh? Knows? Knows what?'

'About us. How we're seeing each other more often.'

'Oh. Right.' Stirring himself, he turned to look at her. 'Yes, I know. We were talking about it when you went for the Easter eggs.'

'You don't approve? Of her knowing, I mean?'

He shrugged and dropped the cigarette in his shirt pocket. 'I don't really care one way or the other, but at the same time, I don't see what business it is of Sheila's.' Brenda was about to reply, when he held up a hand for silence. 'It doesn't matter, Brenda. What we get up to is our affair, no one else's. I can appreciate why you told her, and I don't mind, but I won't have anyone, not even Sheila, sitting in judgement on me… or you.'

'You want to call it a draw, then?' Even as she asked, Brenda was unsure why she was asking.

He did not answer for a moment. When he did, there was no emotion in his voice. 'No. Not unless you do. Do you?'

'Come on, Joe, no one's fooling anyone here. I'm not looking for anything permanent, and I don't think you are. I just need to be sure we're not all going to fall out over it.'

Joe slipped his feet into a pair of soft leather, Wrangler loafers. 'I see no reason why any of us should fall out, and you're right, I'm not looking for anything permanent.' He leaned back against the headboard, hands clasped behind his head, and threw his feet up on the bed. 'You know, one of the big problems between me and Alison was the way she tried to interfere in the business. She wanted it shut half a day during the week and on Saturdays.'

Brenda could not help but agree. 'Sensible woman.'

'No,' Joe argued. 'Not sensible. She wanted the best of both worlds. She wanted the money from the café, but she didn't want the work and responsibilities that went with making the money. And that's the problem with permanent. Listen to me, Brenda, because I know what I'm talking about. I've worked in that café since I left school forty years ago, nigh on. Longer if you count the part time work I did before I left school. I know what it makes. I know how much we'll take on any day, any hour of the week, and I know what I need to do to make the living I want from it. And it's not just me, is it? I have you, Sheila and Lee to pay. You two may not rely on the place for your living, but Lee does. When you start fooling around with the opening hours, you threaten the reliability and stability of the business, and that could see all of us out of work.'

Brenda was puzzled. 'Was there a purpose behind that little lecture?'

'Yes. You. You're not altogether different to Alison. You like a good time, you like time off work to have a good time. And I've never yet stopped either of you from taking a day off here and there. But if we were thinking of something permanent, you and me, that would have to change, and with that change comes instability; the same instability which sent Alison off to Tenerife. What we have now is fine. It's fun, it's satisfying, but I'm in no rush to move it forward.'

Brenda checked her watch. 'Good. Because that's just the way I feel, too.' She smiled encouragingly at him. 'It's almost six and time we were getting down to dinner.'

Rolling from the mattress, he picked up his gilet, slipped his tobacco and lighter into the pockets. 'I hate eating this early.'

'No choice, Joe. The Neil Diamond tribute starts at eight and we have to get there.'

Checking that he had everything, picking up his cagoule, he opened the door and ushered her out.

'You know Joe,' she said as they waited for the lift, 'I never realised how much you truly know about the Lazy Luncheonette.'

He frowned. 'It's a nightmare sometimes. Competition is increasing. We have takeaways on every other corner of the street, the drivers are always under pressure to get on with their work instead of spending their time in the café, a lot of the young kids don't even know what a full English breakfast is, and the retail park draws more passing trade from us every day. I have to know everything.'

The lift arrived. Joe opened the gates and let Brenda enter first.

'You're not just a pretty face, are you?' She watched his wrinkled features screw up as he closed the gates. 'In fact, you're not a pretty face at all.'

Chapter Eight

With the last chords of the final number still reverberating around the hall, a huge round of applause erupted for Nathan Webb, and Joe checked his watch. As the applause died off, people stood and began to file from the rows of seating to the exit aisles.

The show had been excellent. Even Joe had admitted during the interval that it was the perfect aid to digestion after the pepper crusted filet mignon they had enjoyed for dinner at the Leeward. Starting with *America*, concluding with *Crackling Rosie* and a reprise of *America*, Nathan Webb had spent almost two hours on stage running through a repertoire which included all Neil Diamond's greatest hits, with other numbers from artists like Frank Sinatra, Matt Munro and Engelbert Humperdinck.

Aged only about thirty, tall and dark haired, Nathan dressed like Neil Diamond, right down to the dark blue, spangled shirt.

'But he doesn't look much like him,' Joe had noted during a twenty-minute interval which had given them time to visit the toilets and grab a quick drink.

'He sounds like him, though,' Sheila had commented. 'I recall Peter and I went to see the *real* Neil Diamond in Manchester about fifteen years ago.' She gave a heavenly sigh. 'A wonderful evening.'

The second half of the show had proved just as lively, as Nathan, accompanied by a guitarist, drummer, and backing tapes, picked up the pace. Towards the end of the show, some people were dancing in the aisles in front of the stage, until the final number when he took the accolades.

'Quarter past ten,' Joe said as he shuffled along the line of seats in row G. 'We still have time for a couple of beers when we get back to the Leeward.'

'Make mine a Campari,' Brenda said.

Waiting for Les Tanner and Sylvia Goodson to move into the crowded aisle ahead of her, Sheila looked back over her shoulder. 'And I think a nice drop of brandy would serve as a nightcap.'

'Sounds like it's my round again,' Joe commented.

'Really, Joe, I thought when you said we had time, I thought you were inviting us.'

Joe glanced at his watch again, then at the slow moving wedge of people leaving the hall. 'At this rate, we may have to think again. It'll be midnight before we get out of here. Hey, Les, get a bloody move on, will you?'

'We're doing our best, Murray.'

'Some of us are thirsty. Pretend it's Sword Beach and you're trying to batter your way through the German defences.'

Tanner cast a bilious eye on Joe. 'One of these days, Murray, I'll demonstrate a bayonet charge on you.'

The line shuffled forward, and at length, after some delay, they emerged into the Winter Gardens lobby area.

Joe checked his watch again. 'A snifter here, or at the Leeward?'

'It's not half past yet, Joe, and the bar at the Leeward is open until eleven.'

'The Leeward it is, then.'

Joe stepped out into the warm night, where the departing crowds thinned, going their separate ways. He turned right and walked briskly across the front of the Winter Gardens, towards the busy, open seating area of *The View* bar. Sheila and Brenda were several yards behind, following at a more sedate pace, talking between themselves, casting satisfied eyes on the vista across the bay towards the lights of the Grand Pier.

He was so intent on getting back to the Leeward for a final drink or two, that he hardly noticed the two untidily dressed men leaning on the wall at the far end of the Winter Gardens' bar. As he drew near they detached themselves, strode purposefully out onto the pavement, rushed him, grabbed him, and while he shouted a protest, dragged him around the corner.

His heart beating wildly, he could hear Sheila and Brenda calling out for help, and the sound of Brenda's high heels clicking hurriedly on the pavements reached him.

'Get your sodding hands off me,' he yelled.

An unshaven face, the breath reeking of stale beer and tobacco, came close to his. 'You don't like it down here, push off back to Sanford, where you belong.'

'Will you let me go, you moron?'

'Soon as you decide to mind your own business, *Yorkie*.'

'Get off me, dipstick.'

'Looks like he ain't learning the lessons.'

The sound of more feet echoed in Joe's head as he prepared for a hiding.

Two smartly dressed doormen appeared ahead of Sheila and Brenda. The unshaven face took one look at them and said to his pal, 'Scram.' Glaring at Joe again, he growled, 'You ain't heard the last of this… *Yorkie*.'

Releasing Joe, he ran off with his pal. The two security men gave chase while Joe's companions looked after him.

'Are you all right, Joe?' Sheila asked

He nodded, but his entire body trembled. 'What the hell did I do so wrong to bring half this town out against me?'

'Just calm down,' Brenda said, and dug into her bag for her mobile. 'I'll bell George and Owen, see if they're nearby. They can walk with us the rest of the way.'

'I don't need babysitting,' Joe protested.

'Well you could've fooled me,' Brenda retorted, and opening her phone, dialled. She pressed the instrument to her ear. 'George? It's Brenda. Where are you? Joe's just been attacked and we…' She trailed off and listened. Joe could hear the tinny sound of music coming through her phone. 'I don't care if you've trapped off with Miss World, we need some help here… what use is Les Tanner?' She listened again and eventually snapped, 'I won't forget this, George Robson.'

With that, she shut the phone and dropped it back in her bag. 'They're in a club, somewhere, and on a promise with a couple of local tarts.'

'Leave them to it, Brenda,' Joe urged. He was beginning to feel calmer. 'They haven't come all this way to look after me.' He glanced along the road to the Leeward. 'Look, we've only a coupla hundred yards and we're there. If we stick together, they won't dare come for us.'

The doormen came walking back from the rear of the Winter Gardens, taking between themselves. When they reached the three companions, they shrugged.

'Sorry, sir,' said the taller of the pair. 'They got away. Are you all right?'

Joe nodded. 'Feathers a bit ruffled, that's all.'

'May we have your name, sir?' the second asked. 'So we can report it to the police.'

'No need. I'll be seeing Chief Inspector Feeney in the morning, anyway.'

'We still have to report it. If we could have your name.'

'It's Joe Murray,' Sheila said. While the second doorman began to write it down, she went on, 'We're his friends, and we witnessed the attack. Sheila Riley and Brenda Jump. We're all staying at the Leeward Hotel.'

'Thank you, madam. Now, you're sure you're all right, sir?'

'Yes, yes,' Joe said testily. 'I'm fine. Is that it now? Can we get on back to our hotel?'

Without waiting for them to say more, Joe walked off. After another moment talking to the doormen, they hurried after him.

'You really are rude, Joe,' Sheila berated him. 'Those doormen were only trying to help.'

'And the longer I stay out here, the more nervous I'm going to get. I told them I'd be seeing Feeney tomorrow. I'll report the matter then.'

'You could have been more civil,' Brenda observed.

'Right now, I need a drink. I needed one before, but I need it more now. Can we get on?' He strode on and they scurried to keep up. 'You know who's behind this, don't you? Gil and Diane bloody Shipton, that's who.'

'We don't know that for sure.' Sheila was out of breath trying to keep up with him.

'So you think it's all a coincidence, do you?' Joe's pace did not slacken as he spoke. 'I cross swords with them twice, they threatened me twice, and then I'm physically attacked, and yet it's nothing to do with them.'

'All I'm saying is you have no proof.'

Approaching the Leeward entrance, Joe stopped and faced Sheila. 'You know this business of you talking nonsense? Is it natural, or did you take lessons?'

Her anger began to rise, matching his. 'How dare you—'

'Stop it, the both of you,' Brenda intervened. 'Good God, it's bad enough Joe being attacked like that, without getting at each other's throats. Joe, Sheila is right, you have no evidence, let alone proof, and Sheila, Joe is right, too. We may not know it, but the odds are that the Shiptons arranged it. Now let's get inside.' She nodded at the hotel. 'At least we know we'll be safe in there.' She pushed past them and led the way into the Leeward.

In the bar, Freddie and Hazel were pictures of concern. Hazel supplied Joe with brandy while Freddie asked him what had happened.

Joe told the tale and concluded, 'I'm beginning to think Weston-super-Mare doesn't like me.'

'Which now means that most of England doesn't like him,' Brenda quipped.

Joe scowled at her. 'This is the third time I've been threatened since I got here.'

Brenda chuckled. 'Four if you count the chocolate egg Ginny threw at him.'

Joe rounded on her. 'This isn't funny, Brenda.'

'Oh, lighten up, you miserable old scrote. You're not hurt. You said as much yourself.'

'I agree with Joe,' Freddie said. 'It ain't funny. But you will get mixed up with the Shiptons. I told you earlier, matey, keep your distance they're bad news.'

Joe eyed him suspiciously. 'You sound as if you know them.'

Freddie shrugged easily. 'How much do you know about your customers in that café of yours, Joe?'

'The regulars? Plenty.'

'This is a hotel. We're the same. There are those people we won't take bookings from, and the Shiptons are in that class.'

'Ah.' Joe nodded slowly, as if understanding were seeping through his brain. 'I can't understand it. I come to Weston-super-Mare, some barmpot redhead crosses the road without looking where she's going. An hour or two later, that same redhead is in an argument with Ginny Nicholson, I get hit by a chocolate egg, and the whole world goes crazy. Let me ask you something, Freddie. How much did you know about me before we turned up?'

'I knew you ran a café called the Lazy Luncheonette up north, because that was the return address for the booking. That's about it, really.'

'Yes, well, it's more than anyone else in this town ever knew, until I started speaking to Chief Inspector Feeney. So how did the Shiptons get to know...?' He trailed off as the obvious answer struck him. 'Of course. Someone at the cop shop has been talking out of turn.'

Everyone turned surprised stares on him.

'Where do you get that from, Joe?' Sheila's face was determined and angry.

'I know you don't like to hear the police criticised, Sheila.' He smiled indulgently at Freddie and Hazel. 'Sheila's late husband was a police inspector, and like most coppers, he was beyond reproach. But even so, there are rotten apples in the force. Always have been. Freddie, you know something about the Shiptons. Would they be able to afford to bribe a police officer to get information about me?'

'I don't know 'em that well, mate. They're not from round here. They're Londoners.'

'I'll bet on it, though. They've bought someone in the police. How else would they know that I'm a private investigator in my spare time? Why else would they be so worried about me?' He downed his brandy. 'I'll take it up with Feeney first thing in the morning.'

It was left to Brenda to round off the debate. 'If you're right, you're lucky you got away with only being threatened. They bumped Ginny off. Make sure you're not next.'

* * *

Having phoned Chief Inspector Feeney early, Joe was first to start and finish breakfast the following morning. He had asked Freddie and Hazel if they could serve him early, but even so he finished his bacon and eggs to a chorus of protests from his companions.

'We're going to Bath for the day,' Sheila reminded him as he prepared to leave for the police station.

'Yes. And?'

Keith leaned over from a table behind them. 'So we're leaving at a quarter past nine whether you're on the bus or not.'

Joe glared. 'Who pays your bloody wages? You'll do as you're told and while I'm not there, Sheila and Brenda will give you the instructions.' Satisfied that he had put the driver in his place, he said to Sheila, 'I'm meeting Feeney at eight forty-five. That's in…' he checked his watch. 'Twenty minutes. I'll be as quick as I can with her. I'll bell you the minute I come out of the police station, and arrange for Keith to pick me up somewhere.'

Sheila sipped her tea. 'If the members complain, I'm not making excuses for you.'

'Thanks, Sheila. That's the kind of support I love.'

Joe hurried from the Leeward, out into the bright, sunny morning, and hurried along the promenade and through the town centre, arriving at the police station five minutes before his planned meeting with Chief Inspector Feeney.

As he did so, he mentally arranged the information he had to give her in chronological order, beginning with the overheard conversation in The Prince, and ending with the attack at the Winter Gardens, and his conclusions on the matter. He had lain awake into the early hours trying to make sense of it, but had been unable to. It was as if the Shiptons suspected him of knowing something, but he knew nothing.

He said as much to Feeney when they finally settled in her office.

'I took the picture, as you know, and all right so maybe I shouldn't have been listening in on their conversation in the pub, but it's not like I learned anything from it that is key to the issue. Ginny Nicholson wasn't even mentioned.'

The chief inspector looked tired, as if she had been on the tiles the night before. As Joe told her of the events in The Prince, she struggled to suppress a yawn, and eventually she apologised for it. 'It might make more sense than you think, Joe,' she said after apologising for her fatigue. 'Has it occurred to you that Virginia Nicholson may have been the other woman and that Diane murdered her?'

'No, it hadn't,' Joe admitted, 'but as I think about it, there's not a lot of sense in it. Diane wasn't bothered about Gil and what he gets up to. It was the particular woman she was complaining of, and her threat was against Gil, not the woman. She would screw him up, not her.' Clear logic occurred to him. 'And, if it was Ginny, why was there an argument at all? She was already dead when I overheard them.'

Feeney nodded and yawned again. 'You're right, of course. Forgive me, Joe. My brain isn't feeling well this morning. It's obvious then that whatever is going on hinges on the identity of this other woman, but we don't have a clue who she is. All right. You said you had more to tell me.'

Joe went into an account of the previous evening's events outside the Winter Gardens. When he had finished, he said, 'It seems clear to me that the Shiptons set this up. There aren't that many people in Weston who know anything about me. In fact, make that none at all, with the exception of you and your people. I think you have a leak in your ranks.'

She shook her head. 'Not impossible, but in this case, it would have to be Sergeant Holmes, and I can vouch for hm. He's the only other officer who knows about you. I've worked with him for years. He has my complete faith.' She was about to go on when the telephone rang. 'Excuse me.' She picked up the receiver. 'Chief Inspector

Feeney.'

There was a long pause while she listened to the caller. Eventually, she said, 'Who is this?'

Again there was a pause.

'Really, if you're not prepared to identify yourself, I don't see how...'

Feeney trailed off and listened again. 'I see. Well, thank you. I'll take it into consideration.' She replaced the receiver and smiled apologetically at Joe. 'Sorry about that. People ring in all the time with information and they expect us to take it without some form of corroboration such as a name and address.'

'I thought that was the idea of Crimestoppers.'

'Precisely. Now, let's get back to your theory, Joe. It's not beyond the bounds of possibility that our people speak out of turn. I don't say it's deliberate, but it happens. In this case, however, the only person who knows anything about you is Sergeant Holmes and, as I said, I can vouch for him.'

'What about that bobby in the park yesterday? Constable Tetlow?'

'He knows only your name and address, and he even logged that as the Leeward Hotel, not Sanford, West Yorkshire. He doesn't know you've been, er, poking your nose in. But there's something else, Joe. Something I haven't told you, yet.'

'Oh yes?'

Feeney was silent for a long moment. It was as if she was debating whether she should tell him anything. Eventually, she came to a decision. 'I already knew about the attack on you at the Winter Gardens. The security team phoned it in last night. We had Shipton and the Badgers in for questioning. In fact that's why I'm so tired. We were questioning them until two this morning. Gil Shipton admits the earlier confrontation in the Winter Gardens, when your camera was broken, and he admits he faced up to you in The Prince, but all of them deny any involvement in the attack on you. They insist they have not set anyone on you.'

Joe laughed. 'You questioned them half the night after someone attacked me? Isn't that a bit O-T-T?'

'That wasn't the reason we had them in, Joe. We just threw that in as a means of adding to the pressure.'

'Pressure?'

Feeney nodded. 'Diane Shipton. We were at her flat last night where we found her dead.'

Chapter Nine

Joe felt the colour drain from his face. 'Dead?'

Feeney reached for the telephone. 'I'll get you a cup of tea.' There was a brief pause before she gave muttered instructions over the phone, then replaced the receiver. Clasping her hands in front of her, resting on her forearms, she went on, 'We had a report from her neighbours at about half past nine last night. The TV was suddenly playing very loudly. They hammered on the door, couldn't get an answer. They became concerned and called us out. Our lads got there about fifteen minutes later and found her dead. Blunt force trauma to the back of the head.' The chief inspector opened and spread her hands. 'I'm not saying she, or more likely her family, didn't order that pair to warn you off. They may well have been involved, but Diane wasn't around to see whether the instruction had been carried out. She was dead a good half hour before you were threatened. And, of course, the others denied any attack on you.'

'Never mind my attackers. Why the TV? Drowning out the noise of her being murdered?'

Feeney nodded. 'That's the way we see it.'

'Oh, well, it's obvious, then, isn't it? Gil has had enough, so he decided to get rid of her altogether. She was probably giving him lip after he decided to warn me off, he decided he'd had enough and brained her.'

There was a knock at the door and Constable

Tetlow entered with two beakers of tea. When he had gone again, and Joe was settled with a beaker, Feeney finally answered.

'You may be right, but we have no direct evidence of Gil's involvement. Quite the opposite, in fact.' Feeney sipped her tea. 'Gil, Terry Badger and Elaine have alibis for the time of the killing. They were in the bar of the Castle Hotel, and the landlord has confirmed it.'

Joe felt deflated. He swallowed a mouthful of tea. 'So, what you're saying is you may have been barking up the wrong tree all along?'

'We're not ruling out anything, Joe. It's possible that Gil and Terry have brought pressure to bear on the landlord of the Castle Hotel to verify their alibis. I wouldn't put it past them. Sergeant Holmes will be out there again, this morning, to question him, while we have the Badgers and Gil in for questioning. And we'll be pushing Gil on the information you've given us.' She wagged a disapproving finger at him. 'You really shouldn't have put yourself at risk like that, you know.'

Joe shrugged. 'I got away with it.' He laughed sharply. 'By the skin of my teeth, but...' His smile was slowly replaced with a puzzled frown. 'I've done quite a bit of work with the police up and down the country, you know, but this one takes the biscuit. I've never come across anything so complicated. The motives are all to hell and no notion. Tell me, what do you think Diane has hidden that's so important to her husband?'

'I think the same as you. I think it's a detailed account of their activities over the last ten years.

Think about it, Joe. If you're working hand in glove with other people, you have to keep track of the money you're making. As a former journalist, Diane would keep meticulous records. They may be encrypted, they may be *en clair*, as it were, but as you said, they'll almost certainly be password protected.' Feeney chewed at her lip. 'It would help if we knew who Gil's other woman was.'

'I can see the sense in that. You might get some idea of why Diane was so set against it. Would the Met know?'

'We've asked for any information they may have.' Feeney beamed upon him. 'We're not ungrateful, Joe, but I think you've done your bit. Above and beyond the call of duty. Right now we are looking for person or persons unknown in both cases... although...' She trailed off, a thoughtful look coming across her features. Picking up the telephone she dialled and waited a moment before saying, 'It's Chief Inspector Feeney, in Weston. Can you give me a comparison between the weapon used on Virginia Nicholson and the one used on Diane Shipton?' There was a brief pause. 'I know that. I'm not asking for a full post mortem analysis. A simple comparison will do.'

There was another pause and Joe could hear the complaining voice at the other end of the call.

'All I'm asking is whether the same weapon could have been used in both killings.' Feeney paused again and listened. Then, with an exasperated, 'Thank you,' she put the receiver down. 'Nitpicking bloody doctors.'

Joe raised his eyebrows.

'It was something that occurred to me as I was speaking to you just now,' Feeney explained. 'We were told that Ginny Nicholson was killed with a metal implement, and judging by the wound it was a heavy, large sized spanner.'

'The type a mechanic might use?' Joe asked.

She shook her head. 'No... well, that is, most mechanics would have one in their tool kit, but it would be rare that they would need one. This is more like the kind of heavy duty equipment a civil or marine engineer might need. Or someone who repairs lorries. That kind of thing.'

'Well if it belonged to someone like that, there'd be traces of oil or grease on the spanner and it would have some on the wound. Hasn't the pathologist confirmed that, yet?'

'We haven't had the full report yet.' Feeney cast a cynical nod at the phone. 'Which is what that idiot was trying to tell me. It's Easter weekend, Joe. We don't actually shut down, but we certainly slow down, just like any other organisation.'

'A mechanic or engineer? Does Gil Shipton fit the bill?'

'No,' Feeney replied. 'He's a career criminal. So, too, is Terry Badger, but he did start out by ringing and stripping stolen cars.'

'So he might have that kinda toolkit,' Joe reasoned. 'Why would he do that for Diane?'

'Dynamics,' the chief inspector explained. 'The Met's report on the hierarchy of this band of thieves indicates that it's quite rigid. Diane was the source, she and her sister were the blackmailers,

Gil and Terry, the heavies, but Terry followed Gil's orders. Always has done. It could be that Gil ordered Terry to deal with both Virginia and Diane.'

The chief inspector finished her tea, Joe did likewise.

'But we're speculating.' She smiled again. 'Now here's what I want you to do, Joe. Go out and forget all about it. Enjoy the rest of your stay in Somerset. Have a smashing day in Bath. Help your lady friends with their Easter bonnets, but forget about Ginny Nicholson, the Shiptons and the Badgers, and above all have a good time. That's what Weston was designed for.'

He stood and shook hands. 'You've got it.'

* * *

Stepping out of the police station into bright sunshine, Joe first checked his watch and read 9.20. He took out his mobile and rang Brenda.

'Where are you at?' he asked.

'We're just getting on the bus, now. Where are you?'

'Outside the police station.' He began walking along. 'I'll walk to the main road. There's a parade of shops there. Have Keith pick me up there.'

'Roger, dodger. But get a move on. Keith reckons it's about an hour and a quarter to Bath.'

'I'll be there. Stop worrying.'

He put the phone away and ambled along, his mind running over the incident at the Winter Gardens the previous evening.

Joe Murray was no stranger to arguments. He had them all the time in the Lazy Luncheonette, but he was king of the castle up there. He had even faced threats of physical violence in his café, but the presence of his nephew, Lee, was always enough to persuade the would-be assailants to back off. Lee, a former prop forward, was one of life's gentle giants, but his sheer size was enough to worry most people.

He had back up here, too. George and Owen had dealt with the Shiptons and the Badgers first time around, and the Winter Gardens security team had helped persuade the attackers to back off.

It was the why that puzzled Joe. He could perhaps understand Gil Shipton's attitude to the photographs, but why chase Joe down in the Winter Gardens? It made no sense and he said as much to his two companions when he finally took his seat on the bus ten minutes later.

Ignoring his safety belt, and sitting side-saddle in the jump seat, so he could talk to them, he told Sheila and Brenda of his conversation with Chief Inspector Feeney. After they had responded with due surprise bordering on shock, he went on with his speculations on the personal attacks. 'Why am I getting all this hassle? It's not like I actually know anything, is it?'

'They don't know that, Joe,' Sheila pointed out. 'I remember Peter telling that quite often, in cases of intimidation, the victim didn't know anything or if they did, they weren't aware of what they knew.'

'No, look, you're not with me. Diane was

murdered last night while we were watching the Neil Diamond lookalike. They sent those bods after me, so it's obvious they knew I was at the show. What could I possibly know about Diane's death? What do I know about Ginny's murder? Come to that, I don't know too much about the business between Diane and Gil. I only overheard a brief bit of their conversation in that pub, and they weren't getting into names or anything, and the cops were already onto it.'

'No, Joe. You're getting your timing mixed up.' She raised mock eyes overhead. 'Typical man.' Grinning at Joe, she went on, 'You overheard them yesterday afternoon, the police didn't interview them until Diane's body was found. If they were going to hassle you, it would have been arranged before Diane was killed.'

Joe turned to face forward again as Keith pulled out to pass a slow-moving lorry on the steep climb up the Clevedon Gorge. As their driver pulled back into the nearside lane, he turned again to face his companions. 'You're wrong.'

Brenda shrugged. 'We would be, wouldn't we?'

'You are. I know you are. But I can't think why.'

Sheila smiled benignly, the way one would smile upon a simple-minded relative. 'Is this a famous, "I'm missing something" Joe Murray moment?'

'It is. I don't see what Gil and the Badgers have to gain from braining Diane... well, I do. He obviously wanted rid of her. But whatever she has hidden, and wherever it's hidden, it's still out there. There is still the danger that the information, assuming that's what it is, will come to light.'

'True,' Sheila agreed, 'but is it any use without Diane's testimony?'

Joe grunted. 'Have to admit, I hadn't thought of that. The police would need verification from the victims, and they won't be in a big hurry to come forward.'

'It seems to me that Diane was killed for two possible reasons, then,' Brenda chimed in. 'To get her out of Gil's hair or to shut her up, or possibly both.'

'And why was Ginny killed?' Joe demanded.

His question was greeted with a silence punctuated only by the rumble of the bus and Keith's occasional remonstration with other drivers as the Easter traffic thronged the motorway.

When Keith pulled over onto the M4 interchange, to turn east for Bath, Sheila finally spoke up. 'Perhaps she was thinking of going to the police, and they decided to shut her up.'

Joe disagreed again. 'Ginny's argument with Diane happened when? Two o'clock Thursday afternoon. If she was gonna complain to the cops, she'd have done it on Thursday. Yet she didn't or Feeney would have told me. The first the police knew of the argument was when we told them yesterday morning.'

'Maybe she only threatened to go to the police and that was enough,' Brenda suggested.

Again Joe would not hear it. 'The Shiptons

and the Badgers are no fools when it comes to dealing with the law. The only person guilty of anything on Thursday was Ginny when she threw the chocolate egg at Diane… and missed. They didn't have to kill her. All they had to do was brazen it out.' He injected more urgency into his voice. 'I can see the sense in what you're saying, but it's all too pat, and there's something missing.'

'The document or documents Diane has tucked away,' Brenda said with a smile.

Joe's features twisted into a mask of blind anger. 'Not physically missing. I mean there's something missing from the argument. It doesn't quite hang together. I just said the Shiptons and the Badgers are not stupid. For them to have done all this means they've done too much. They may have believed that killing Ginny and Diane was necessary, but in that case, why warn me off? Why not go for me with an engineer's spanner? Why not put me out of the game for good, too? Gil would have had the chance when I came out of that pub yesterday, and those two clowns last night could have done worse if they'd wanted.' He shrugged again. 'It just doesn't quite hang together.'

They left the debate there and while watching the fields of Avon pass by, Sheila and Brenda engaged in chatter on the prospect of Bath now less than half an hour ahead of them.

Joe sat facing forward and even put his seat belt on when Keith grumbled that there was a police patrol car coming up on the outside of them. It passed with barely a glance at them, and soon their driver pulled off the motorway and dropped onto the twisting and hilly A46 for the final, eleven miles into Bath.

While the rest of the passengers oohed and aahed at their first sight of the old city in the valley below them, Joe's febrile mind flipped over and over the last thirty-six hours, seeking that elusive something he was missing. It was always the way. A vital spark that would put him on the right track, but like a finger prodding him for attention in the midst of a pushing crowd, it evaded him, lost in a welter of impression, theories and counter-theories.

Dropping down the hill into the city centre, Keith followed the inner ring road to the official coach park by the riverside, where under the guidance of an attendant, he reversed into an empty slot alongside other coaches, and climbed off.

Relieved at having something to take his mind off Weston-super-Mare and the murders, Joe picked up the PA microphone.

'All right people, here's the deal. There are official tour guides here in Bath, and one of them will be getting on the bus in a minute or two. He'll guide Keith round the city, and stop here and there to give you a brief talk on what you're seeing. It doesn't come free. If you're staying on the bus, it costs six pounds a head. If you don't wanna pay it, and you'd rather go into the city centre and find your own way round, you're welcome to, but if you're staying on, I need your money up front.'

He removed his cap, took out his own wallet

and dropped a twenty in the cap to cover his, Sheila's and Brenda's fare, then made his way along the aisle collecting from the passengers.

Half way down, he had to wriggle past George and Owen who were preparing to get off.

'You don't want the tour?'

George scowled. 'If I wanna hear some boring old fart prattling on about the bloody Roman plumbing, I'll have a couple of beers with Alec Staines.'

'Oi. I heard that,' Alec called out from a few seats behind. 'And I'm a painter and decorator, not a bleeding plumber.'

'Same difference,' George replied. 'Staying on the bus is wasting valuable drinking time.'

'Back here for half past four,' Joe ordered and carried on along the aisle collecting the fares.

Ten minutes later, Keith started the engine again and pulled out of the car park, while the guide introduced himself as Tony Allington, and showed off his blue badge, which he assured everyone, was the best way of recognising an officially appointed tour guide.

For the next hour he guided Keith around the outer city, even out onto rural roads, asking him to stop occasionally, where he would point out the landmarks, and allow the passengers to get off in one or two places, so they could take photographs. Joe, his focus more on the tour than the Weston killings, was as busy as anyone with his Sony DSLR, camera.

Coming back into the city, when Keith stopped at traffic lights, Tony pointed further down the hill to the Jane Austen Centre, where a man dressed completely in regency attire, greeted visitors. He asked Keith to turn right into Queen's Square and took them twice round it, pointing out the varied architecture – Palladian and Grecian – of the different sides, and gave them a brief lecture on the life and times of John Wood and John Pinch, before directing Keith out of the square along the A4, and up Marlborough Lane for their final stop on Royal Avenue where they could take in the view of the Royal Crescent.

Keith parked ahead of a police patrol car, and everyone, including the driver, disembarked, for the short walk up a broad path, and from there they had a magnificent view of the whole crescent. While Tony gave them a potted history of the place, Joe began taking pictures, swapping lenses for different close ups and panoramic shots.

Struggling to see his photographs in the strong sunlight, he backed under the shade of a tall tree and studied the images on the camera's tiny screen.

'Good,' he muttered. 'I'll put a couple of those in the next newsletter.'

He switched off the camera, detached the lens, and dropped it in the pocket of his gilet. Looking around, he realised the group had moved off, retracing their steps back to the bus.

He turned to follow them and at that moment, two men grabbed him and threw him to the ground.

'Hey!'

Joe's head spun. He looked up into two faces,

almost blocked out by the sunlight, and vaguely recognised them from the night before.

One of them drew back a solid fist and prepared to deliver it. Joe closed his eyes waiting for the blow.

It never came. There was a sudden flurry of activity around him, shouts and cries, most of them unintelligible. Cautiously he opened his eyes again and saw the two attackers now restrained by several police officers, a smiling Chief Inspector Feeney stood nearby.

'What the hell...?'

Joe struggled to his feet and noticed that some of his friends, amongst them Sheila, Brenda and Keith, were hurrying back up from the bus to see what the fuss was all about.

'Hello, Joe,' Feeney greeted him.

'What... I don't, er, I don't understand.'

'You remember the phone call I took while you were with me this morning? The call where the informer wouldn't identify herself? It was a tip off. The caller told me that these two would come for you here, so we followed you. In fact, we passed you on the motorway, and we've been following your bus all over Bath. While your driver was going round Queen's Square a couple of time, we guessed this would be your next and last port of call, so if they were going to attack you, it would be here.'

'Not in the city centre?' Joe asked.

'Too crowded down there.'

'Are you all right, Joe?' Sheila asked, her face a mask of concern.

'Yeah, no problem, but I'm beginning to wish I'd never heard of Weston-super-Mare and Bath.' He turned aggrieved features on Feeney. 'Couldn't you have nicked them earlier? I mean they must have been following us, too.'

'Not that we noticed.' Feeney waved a hand around her. 'This is the Royal Crescent, Joe, possibly the most famous street in Bath. No matter where else they go, every tour of the city stops here. They knew they'd find you here sometime today. And we couldn't pick them up earlier. We didn't know who they were.' She aimed a finger at the two attackers. 'Are they the same pair who went for you in the Winter Gardens last night?'

Joe nodded. 'They are. Lucky for them that I chose to take the tour, then, rather than go for a pint with George and Owen.'

'Who?' Feeney asked.

'Two friends. So what'll you do with them now?'

She smiled on the two men. 'Take them back to Weston-super-Mare and have a little chat with them, see if we can't get to the bottom of this business.' She chuckled at Joe. 'You carry on and enjoy yourself. I don't think you're in any more danger.'

* * *

'Somebody obviously means business to send them all this way after me,' Joe grumbled. 'What the hell is it I'm supposed to know?'

'I don't think you know anything, Joe,' Sheila

insisted, and leaned to one side while a waitress served her. 'I think they're just afraid you know something.'

An hour had passed since the incident on the Royal Crescent. Keith had brought them back to the centre of Bath and the coach park, where everyone left the bus for an afternoon walking around the city centre.

After wandering through streets where Roman, Regency and modern mingled freely, they had found their way to Sally Lunn's House, reportedly the oldest in Bath, in one of the narrow streets near the Abbey. After visiting the Kitchen Museum, where Brenda commented that the 16th century ovens reminded her of the kitchen in the Lazy Luncheonette, they secured a table in the dining room and ordered three Bath Cream Teas; half a Sally Lunn Bun, toasted, and topped with cinnamon butter and clotted cream.

Typically, Joe had complained about the prices.

'The thick end of twenty quid for three toasted teacakes and cream? It's daylight robbery. How much do we charge at the Lazy Luncheonette? Seven and a half quid, the lot. That's value, that is.'

'Yes, Joe, but our toasted teacakes come with a squirt of supermarket cream from a can.'

'And you charge another fifty pee per squirt,' Sheila pointed out.

Brenda added to his angst. 'And your tea is served in cracked beakers, not best china.'

'Plus you don't have a kitchen museum,'

Sheila reminded him. 'Instead, you have a widescreen TV showing awful daytime programmes.'

'And you don't have waitress service.'

Spotting an opening Joe leapt upon it. 'Sheila delivers the meals.'

'Four at a time,' she said. 'I don't get a fancy pinny, only a mucky tabard.'

'Can you imagine what the draymen would make of you in a black skirt, white blouse, dark stockings and a frilly apron? They'd be demanding a strip show.'

'In that case, you'd have to make Brenda your official temptress… I mean waitress.'

To head off Brenda's sudden enthusiasm for the idea, Joe shifted the focus to the events on the Royal Crescent.

Brenda tucked into her toasted bun and licked cream from her fingers. 'Did you tell Feeney about the fake Easter egg in the Winter Gardens, Joe?'

He sipped tea. 'No. What's to tell? There's nothing in it.'

'I thought we had this debate yesterday,' Sheila complained. 'You're assuming there's nothing in the egg, Joe, but you can't be certain, and let's be honest about it; the heat has certainly gone up since Gil caught you trying to photograph Diane.'

'And caught you earwigging their conversation in The Prince.'

'I know all that,' Joe protested, and bit into his bun. His face wrinkled in disgust. 'That is awful. What the hell have they done with it? I think I'd rather have a Lancashire oven bottom muffin.'

'It's probably the cinnamon butter,' Sheila said. 'You're not used to such delicacies.'

Joe sniffed. 'Pardon me while I ask for some bread and dripping. This doesn't make total sense. There's something missing.'

'A Yorkshire pudding?' Brenda asked.

'Not with the food. The Weston business.'

'You keep saying this, Joe. Have you worked out what it is, yet?'

Joe took another bite of his bun to enhance his scowl. 'If I knew what it was, I wouldn't be going on about it, would I?'

From the Sally Lunn House, they toured the streets. The women bought souvenirs and Joe picked up a decorative ashtray for his apartment. By three o'clock, they were in the Roman Bath Museum, having decided that the queue for the lower baths was too long.

Instead, they looked down from the street level galleries on the green waters of the Sacred Spring, and all three sampled the waters on offer.

Joe grimaced at the sulphur. 'Tastes as bad as the beer at the Miner's Arms, and it's almost as bad as that bun.'

Brenda laughed. 'You really are a misery, Joe.' She waved her arms around the room. 'When this place was built by the Romans, Sanford was a mud hut on the banks of the River Aire.'

The light lit in Joe's mind. 'Of course. That's it.'

The two women exchanged knowing glances.

'Go on, Joe,' Sheila invited.

'The idiots who attacked me last night, and again today. Last night, they said to me, 'get back to Sanford'. Gil Shipton doesn't know I'm from Sanford, and neither did his wife. In fact, there's only one party who does know.'

'Who?'

'Freddie bloody Delaney.'

Chapter Ten

When Keith stopped the bus outside the Leeward, Joe was first off as always, but even though the sun was shining this time, he still hurried into reception seeking Freddie Delaney.

Throughout the eighty-minute journey from Bath, he had sat in his jump seat fuming, occasionally urging Keith to get his foot down.

The driver's response varied from, 'This is as fast as the bus goes,' to waving through the windscreen and asking, 'What do you want me to do about all these cars? Leapfrog them?'

Inside the hotel, he found no trace of Freddie or Hazel. A barman told him he had not seen Freddie all day, but Hazel was supervising the preparation of the dining room for the imminent evening meal. When Joe tried to get into the dining room, he found his way blocked by a burly waiter.

He was arguing with the waiter when Sheila and Brenda arrived and dragged him into the bar.

'For God's sake get a grip of yourself, Joe,' Brenda urged while Sheila bought him a half of lager.

'Me get a grip of myself? Freddie's goons have already had a grip of me. Well, now I'm losing it and I'll carry on losing it until I see him.'

'Just calm down,' Sheila advised. 'The way you're going on you'll have a stroke or a heart attack.'

'I—'

'You don't know that Freddie sent those men after you,' Brenda interrupted before Joe could protest further. 'And even if he did, may I remind you that he's twice your size.'

'Then he'll fall a lot harder than me,' Joe snapped.

'How? Are you going to punch him in the kneecaps? Grow up, Joe.'

His response was a furious roar. 'I want explanations.'

'He has some questions to answer, I'll grant you,' Sheila observed, 'but losing your temper will not get you anywhere, Joe.'

'He's been taking the pi—'

'Joe…' there was a warning edge to Brenda's voice and he moderated his language.

'He's been taking the mick with us since yesterday morning. All along we're blaming the Shiptons and the Badgers and it was him. He even has the tools.' He waved at the bar. 'He has this bloody great spanner for changing barrels. I saw him with it the first night we were here. Feeney told me it's the kind of weapon which was used to kill both Ginny and Diane Shipton. Wouldn't you be angry?'

'Yes,' Sheila agreed, 'but not to the point you are. Let's try and stay a little calmer, eh? See what we sort out when we get to speak to him.'

'Or you could call the cops,' Brenda suggested.

'Not until I've confronted him.' Joe fumed some more and took out his tobacco to roll a cigarette. Unable to control his shaking hands, he dug deeper into his pocket and came out with a rolling machine.

'I often wondered why you carried that,' Brenda observed conversationally.

'It's for when I'm fit to strangle someone.' He held out a shaking hand, then spread tobacco along the innards of the machine and rolled it before inserting a cigarette paper and completing the job. 'An awful lot has occurred to me while I was on the bus, and when I see him, he gets both barrels.'

Brenda smiled. 'Without a filter tip?'

Joe was about to tackle her levity when Hazel stepped into the bar, looked around and made for them. She appeared pale and distressed, her brow furrowed with lines of worry. 'I believe you wanted a word, Mr Murray?' The voice was firm and businesslike, but there was an edginess to it, which spoke volumes to Joe.

'Not you. I wanna speak to your old man, and I don't want any excuses. Get him in here, now.'

'I'm sorry. He's not here.'

'I just said, no excuses.'

Hazel made an obvious effort to hide her distress. 'I said, he's not here.'

'What time will he be back?'

'I don't know.'

Joe's anger tipped the scales once more. 'If anyone ever mentions Weston-super-Mare or the bloody Leeward Hotel again, I won't be responsible. Just knock it off, woman, and tell me when—'

'He's not here,' Hazel interrupted. She glanced around the room. 'I need a cigarette.

Would you care to step outside where we can talk without my staff listening in?'

She did not wait for Joe to answer, but turned smartly, and walked out.

Nonplussed by her actions, Joe grabbed his beer and followed. The two women checked with each other, and they, too, followed.

Hazel sat under one of the parasols, a light, offshore breeze ruffling her blonde hair, the glow of the setting sun picking out the lines of worry in her features. She lit a cigarette and drew deeply on it as Joe and his two companions joined her.

Blowing the smoke out with a long hiss, she said, 'Freddie has gone. He left in the early hours of the morning before the police could arrest him for Diane Shipton's murder.'

The announcement drew Joe up short. Brenda shouldered him out of the way to get to Hazel. On the other side, Sheila pushed him even further away.

'When did he leave, Hazel?' Brenda asked.

'I told you. The early hours. He was out last night. He went to see Diane Shipton. Don't ask me why, he wouldn't tell me. When he got to where she was living, he found the street packed with police cars. One of the neighbours told him a woman had been found dead. He knew it was her and he knew he would be blamed, so he came back here. After we closed for the night, we sat up talking about it, and by three this morning, he was gone.' A look of pleading came into her eyes. 'He didn't do it. He wouldn't.'

Brenda half turned to face Joe. 'Well?'

Joe remained unrepentant. Lighting his cigarette, he said, 'Well what? He sent those clowns after me. I know he did. Why? To frighten me off. And why would he want me frightened off? Because he killed her, and he knew I'd probably get to the truth.'

'He didn't kill her, Mr Murray,' Hazel insisted. 'He wouldn't.'

Joe leaned forward. 'He sent those guys after me. Don't deny it. I know he did.'

Diane took a deep breath. 'Yes he did. And when you and your friends scared them off last night, they rang. Late last night. Freddie told them to drop it, they said no way. You made them look fools, and they were out to pay you back. They said they would follow you today. Freddie never wanted them to hurt you. He just wanted to scare you into minding your own business.'

'But he didn't reckon on someone tipping the cops off, did he?'

Joe sat back, triumphant. Hazel glared at him.

'That was me, you idiot. I phoned Feeney and told her.'

'You?'

Hazel dragged on her cigarette again. 'Freddie daren't ring them, so I did. Anonymously.'

Sheila frowned. 'I'm sorry, Mrs Delaney, but I don't understand all this. Your husband must have had dealings with Diane Shipton in the past. Now we know she is... was... a blackmailer. Did she have some hold over Freddie?'

'Of course she did,' Joe cut in. 'Freddie was like Ginny Nicholson, wasn't he, Hazel?'

Sheila and Brenda were stunned by the announcement. Hazel froze for a moment, then slowly, she nodded. 'He's served time in prison, yes. How did you know, Joe?'

'Something Freddie said to me yesterday when we got back from Clifftop Park. He said Diane was not a killer. Now how would he know that? Sure, he could have worked for her or with her, but the minute I realised it was him who sent those thugs after me, it became clear. Diane came here, threatened Ginny, and then Ginny was murdered. She must have threatened Freddie, too. Why? What could she have on him? The same kind of information she had on Ginny. Too right he wanted to scare me off. He didn't want me getting too close because I'd already told him that when it comes to crime, I'm the best.' He took an irritable drag on his smoke. 'And I'm not having this crap about him going out to see Diane and finding the cops there. He went out to get rid of her before she could expose him. Either that or he wanted to know where she kept the information she had on him.'

Hazel crushed out her cigarette. 'Listen to me, Mr Murray. He... did... not... do... it.' She stressed the individual words by driving her index finger into the tabletop.

'We'll see what the cops think about that.'

'You're too late,' Hazel said. 'Feeney and her pal, Holmes were round here earlier. They want to speak to him if and when he shows up.' She glanced at her watch. 'I have to supervise dinner. Could we pick up this conversation later? After the bar has shut? I promise I will tell you everything I know.'

* * *

'Freddie took part in an armed robbery in Bristol. He got fifteen years, served half his sentence, and he was released five years ago. That's when he came to Weston-super-Mare. He was determined he wasn't going back to prison, and since then he's been as good as gold.'

It was coming up to midnight. Still convinced that Hazel was covering up for her husband, Joe had put it to one side, but he was taciturn and throughout dinner and through the two hours of entertainment afterwards. Even after the female singer had called it a night, and his party were enjoying their final drinks of the evening, while Brenda and Sheila joined in the general banter, Joe sat by the window, looking out on a mild, spring evening, barely acknowledging any of his friends.

Hazel had put on a good front. Not her usual, smiling self, but she remained polite and efficient behind the bar, and when they closed for the night, she helped the barman cash up, before sending him home and bringing a tray of drinks across to the windows where she could join the three companions.

Joe's mood still had not improved, and he listened to her with a scowl of cynicism.

Sheila, on other hand, was more sympathetic. 'Someone died during the robbery, didn't they?'

Hazel swallowed a lump in her throat. 'A

security guard unloading the van they robbed. He was shot and died later. Freddie was the wheel man, the driver. He wasn't armed, so he had nothing to do with the killing, but it was enough to give him a long stretch. His three accomplices were given life sentences.' Hazel sighed. 'Something must have happened while he was inside to make him see his life in a different light. I don't know what, and he's never told me, but he became a model prisoner and he was paroled after half his sentence. However, until his fifteen years is complete, he can be sent back to prison at any time for any offence, no matter how trivial.'

'Like setting two thugs onto me. Like bumping off Ginny Nicholson and Diane Shipton.' Joe's bile showed through his gritted response.

'For the umpteenth time, he didn't do it, Mr Murray,' Hazel urged. 'He told me he didn't do it, and I believe him.' Hazel reached behind Joe and threw open a window. Taking out her cigarettes, she said, 'We're not supposed to, but as long as you ladies don't mind?'

Sheila and Brenda shook their heads, and while Hazel lit a cigarette, Joe rolled one.

Blowing a fine steam of smoke at the open window, Hazel demanded, 'Why would my Freddie murder Ginny? They were in the same boat. Both ex-cons, both trying to keep it secret so they could get on with their lives. Freddie and Ginny were friends; no way would he murder her.'

Lighting his cigarette, following Hazel's example and blowing the smoke through the window as if aiming it at the pier lights, Joe struggled with Hazel's announcement. Chief Inspector Feeney had said to him that Ginny was not the only one with a dark secret in the town. A hint, later reinforced by Freddie's own words, that they both had records. And in that respect, it was true that Ginny's murder made no sense: at least not if Freddie committed it.

With no safe answer for Hazel, he diverted attention instead. 'Freddie was trying to scare me off by sending those idiots after me. Scare me off from what? It's not like I know anything.'

'Well I can see a kind of logic to it,' Sheila said. 'What you mean, Hazel, is that if Joe began to poke his nose in, he might inadvertently stumble across Freddie's prison record.'

'Something like that,' Hazel agreed. 'And he did, didn't he?'

'Only because your husband opened his trap,' Joe argued. 'And it still makes no sense to me. What difference does it make me knowing? The police know about him, I'm sure.'

Hazel tutted. 'It's not the police he was worried about. Apart from them, no one knows. We keep it a secret. Can you imagine what it would do to the hotel if people found out? It could ruin us. Remember, Mr Murray, you're a stranger here. We don't know you, you don't know us. If you found out, you could let it slip in all innocence and not realise the damage you were doing. Not only that, but you probably wouldn't care, either. What difference would it make to you? You're two hundred miles away. So what do you care if another seaside hotel goes under through lack of bookings? To my way of thinking, Freddie wanted to keep you out of this Diane Shipton business to stop you turning up his past. All right, all right—' Hazel held up her hands in a gesture of defeat. 'He let it slip, tried to correct it and went the wrong way about it. It was naughty. But he only wanted to scare you, not hurt you. That's why I tipped Feeney off when those two drunken fools decided to teach you a lesson their way.'

A sulking silence fell. Joe and Hazel drew on their cigarettes. Brenda and Sheila fiddled with their drinks. It was as if no one knew which way to go next.

Then Brenda said, 'Diane. Where does she fit into all this?'

'She was blackmailing Freddie the way she blackmailed Ginny,' Joe declared.

Hazel shrugged as eyes fell on her. 'I think you're right, but Freddie wouldn't tell me. I think he knew Diane from when she was a reporter, and I think later on, she got her claws into him, took him for some serious cash. That's probably why he came to Weston-super-Mare in the first place. I'm speculating, because Freddie has never said anything to me about her.'

'You've seen Diane here?' When Hazel denied it with a shake of the head, Joe snorted. 'There you are then.' His voice brimmed with triumph. 'Diane probably killed Ginny, then warned Freddie that it was his turn next if he didn't poppy up. He decided that whatever she would do unto him, he would do unto her, only he did it first. He went out last night and topped her.

End of story.' He took another drag on his smoke and flicked it through the window, sending it spinning, a tiny glow of red in the night, to the patio.

Hazel rose to his challenge. 'You're the alleged detective. Prove it.'

Joe was conscious of all eyes on him, and went on the defensive. 'Me prove it? Why should I? It's nothing to do with me. Other than I think he should be locked up for life... again. And this time, life should—'

'It was nothing to do with you in Lincoln, but it didn't stop you,' Sheila cut in.

'Yes, but—'

'Or Filey,' Brenda added.

'Or Leeds or York,' Sheila said.

'I know, but—'

'Even in Chester it was nothing to do with you, but you dived in because I'd been accused,' Brenda reminded him.

Joe waited for another interjection from his friends. When it didn't come, he went on the attack. 'What I'm getting here is the same nonsense I heard in Lincoln—'

It was as if his voice had become the cue for interruptions. 'And you proved it in Lincoln,' Brenda reminded him.

'It was different,' Joe yelped. 'I didn't have to deal with threats to beat my brains in. I've had nothing but since I got here.'

'I'm telling you he wouldn't do it,' Hazel insisted.

'And you don't know that.'

'I do know it.'

'How?' Joe pressed. 'Oh, don't tell me. It's because you love him and he would never do anything to betray your love.'

'Oh, don't talk bloody nonsense,' Hazel snapped.

'Then explain,' Joe insisted.

Hazel drew an exasperated breath. 'He made mistakes when he was younger. He doesn't make any excuses for them. All right, he keeps it secret, but on the rare occasions that he speaks to me about it, he admits that what he did was wrong. A man died. That man's family had their lives ruined, and at the same time, Freddie ruined his own life. If he could turn back the clock, he would undo it, but he can't. He came to me as a bar cellar man, which is what he was before he turned to robbery. I'd just gone through a divorce, I needed a barman with Freddie's capabilities, I took him on. We fell in love and married two years ago. In all the time he's been with me, he hasn't put a foot wrong, and remember, as matters stand, he can be taken back to prison for the meanest of offences and be made to serve out the rest of his sentence. That's why he's careful to toe the line, stick to the right way. It's also why he disappeared last night.'

Joe was not convinced. 'If he's got such a past, how come he can get a liquor licence?'

'He can't.' Hazel pointed at the sign above the bar carrying her name. 'I'm the licensee, not him.' She urged him with burning eyes. 'You're sidetracking the issue. Feeney doesn't need much to send Freddie back to jail. And if she can conveniently hang this business on him while he's serving the rest of his fifteen-year sentence, so much the better. But you could help. Feeney likes you. She'd listen to you.'

'And then she'd send him back to jail because I think he's guilty,' Joe pointed out.

'Oh, for God's sake, what do I have to do to get through to you?' Hazel ran a frustrated hand through her hair. 'Mr Murray, I don't know what is going on any more than anyone else, but I do know Freddie is not mixed up in it. Right now, he's running for his life. That's all. In his position, you'd probably do the same. But if you're the detective everybody claims you are, you should be able to find who really did kill Diane, and that will prove Freddie innocent.'

Joe glanced up at the clock above the bar. 'It's nearly half past twelve, I'm tired, I need some sleep.'

'And you need to calm down,' Sheila told him.

'And I need to calm down.' He collected his tobacco and stood up. 'I'll think about it.'

* * *

Clad in pale green pyjamas, Brenda emerged from the shower just as Sheila finished making their last cup of tea.

Taking a cup, climbing into bed, Brenda sipped gratefully. 'So what do you think about Hazel and Freddie?'

Placing her cup and saucer on the cabinet

between the twin beds, Sheila, too, climbed under the sheets, and picked up her tea. 'I think it sounds plausible, but I also think she's a woman in love, and blind to the alternatives.'

'That Freddie did kill Diane?'

Sat up in bed, holding her saucer, sipping from the cup, Sheila nodded. 'If Diane was blackmailing him, he may very well take the extreme course of action.' She frowned. 'It's very confusing, isn't it? If we assume that Freddie killed Diane, where does this business between Diane and Gil come into it?'

Brenda laughed. 'I don't suppose Gil was having an affair with Freddie.'

Sheila chuckled. 'I think not. According to Joe's version of events, Diane definitely referred to the other woman as 'her'.' Her features saddened. 'Poor Joe. Getting the brunt of it as usual.'

'He loves it.' Brenda laughed. 'He's the centre of attention, he gets to ply that magic mind of his, and even if he's been threatened, it'll just be another tale for him to tell in his casebooks and over the counter in the Lazy Luncheonette.'

Sheila did not look at Brenda as she spoke. 'And what of you and he? Will that be another tale to tell over the counter of the Lazy Luncheonette.'

Brenda giggled. 'It better not be.' She drank more tea. 'I talked to him about us, yesterday. Told him I'd told you. He's adamant that it's none of your business, but he doesn't mind you knowing. And, like me, he's not after anything permanent. You know Joe. His private life has always been between him and his conscience. We knew nothing of it. I think he'll keep it that way.'

* * *

On the floor above, also sat up in bed with a cup of tea, his laptop resting on his knees, Joe's thoughts were less of his putative relationship with Brenda, and more upon what he perceived as the injustices heaped upon him. He was utterly convinced of Freddie Delaney's guilt in the murder of Diane Shipton, and of her guilt in the murder of Ginny Nicholson, but the problem of Diane's argument with Gil nagged at him.

'I don't believe in coincidence', he could often be heard to say.

Coincidences happened all the time in everyday life, but when they racked up in a murder investigation, they usually amounted to guilt. The argument in the pub pointed the finger squarely at Gil Shipton ridding himself of a liability, but Freddie's actions and reactions to events, indicated his guilt too.

So which one was it?

The word *complicity* struck him. Perhaps Gil and Freddie had got together and decided they were both better without Diane.

How did Freddie know Gil?

Simple: he had known Diane, so it was odds on he had met Gil at some time.

Joe scrolled back through his notes on the laptop seeking something, anything that might point him in the right direction.

He recalled his brief conversation with Freddie on the morning Ginny's body had been found in Clifftop Park. *Take it from someone who knows. Diane Shipton may be a blackmailer, but she's no killer.* There was no escaping the truth, no matter how much Hazel tried to argue against it. Freddie knew Diane well. She *had* blackmailed him. Perhaps Freddie had refused to pay up, so instead of going public with her knowledge, she sent Gil and Terry Badger in to persuade Freddie.

Looking away from the screen, into the darkness of his room, Joe imagined a confrontation between the three men. Gil and Terry Badger were big, muscular men, but so was Freddie. They had done time for violence, Freddie had taken the big one for armed robbery and accomplice to murder. Who would come out on top?

'Even at two to one, you could rule out Freddie winning the fight,' he muttered to himself.

And if that had happened, what price Gil would have come to Freddie here in Weston in a spirit of amelioration, offering a deal that would suit them all? A deal that involved Freddie simply doing away with Diane.

Joe shut down the laptop, climbed out of bed, and tucked it away in its case. He was tired and thoroughly fed up of the whole business. He would talk to Patricia Feeney first thing in the morning, all right, but it would be to persuade her that the man she was looking for was Freddie Delaney.

Chapter Eleven

For Joe, breakfast on Easter Sunday was a sullen affair.

All around him the club members chattered excitedly about the day head, their last in Weston. Sheila and Brenda were deep in a none-too serious conversation with Sylvia Goodson and Les Tanner on the forthcoming Easter Bonnet Parade, and on the table behind them, George Robson and Owen Frickley were arguing the relative merits of football versus rugby league with Alec and Julia Staines.

Chewing his way through a bowl of corn flakes and following with bacon and eggs, Joe remained silent, lost in his own thoughts.

He had been outside, enjoying a smoke at seven thirty, watching the glorious sunny morning develop, and he was one of the first at the table for breakfast, but he had seen no sign of Hazel Delaney. He reasoned that unlike his own establishment, where he had to be there to open up, she had enough staff to cope without her after a late night.

Throughout the meal, his companions tried to draw him into the conversation, but Joe would not have it, leaving Les Tanner, who enjoyed ragging him, plenty of scope for cutting remarks. By 8.45am, he was back outside smoking again. At nine, he rang Feeney and arranged to see her at the police station at ten. As he put his phone away,

Brenda came out into the morning sunshine and sat with him.

'Still got it on you, Joe?'

'I'm all right,' he lied. 'No better, no worse than normal.'

'In that case, we're in for a hell of an Easter Sunday, aren't we? Sheila wants to go to church, I'm trying to get out of it, but the only alternative is sticking with you, and you're colder than a polar bear's backside.'

'There's always George,' Joe suggested. 'I'm sure he can keep you entertained.' Brenda glared thunder at him and he promptly backtracked. 'Sorry. That was below the belt.'

'Right where it was aimed,' she snapped.

'I said I'm sorry.' Joe relit his cigarette. 'Stick with Sheila for the time being. I have to go to the police station.'

'You're going to help prove Freddie innocent?'

He shook his head. 'Nope. Because I don't believe Freddie is innocent. I think he's guilty as hell.'

'But—'

He silenced her with an upraised hand. 'I heard it all last night, I don't wanna hear it again. There are things which don't make sense and I'm seeing Feeney to try to make sense of them. I think Freddie was mixed up with Gil Shipton and I think they may have been working together on it. Feeney will straighten me out. After that, it's your Easter bonnet show, a few beers tonight and, thank God, home tomorrow.' He took another pull on his cigarette. 'No matter what happens, I always enjoy the STAC outings, but I'll be glad when this one is over.'

Brenda reached across the table and touched his hand, a simple gesture of sympathy. 'I'm sorry, Joe. It has been rough for you this time.' She smiled coyly. 'Tell you what, after you've seen madam Chief Inspector, why not take me back to your room and I'll show you a really good time?'

Joe refused to rise to the temptation. 'We'll see.'

Sheila stepped out of the hotel, followed by Sylvia and Les Tanner, Sylvia in her sombre, Sunday best, a heavy coat insulating her against the promise of another warm day, Les looking immaculate in his regimental blazer and tie.

'There you both are,' Sheila said. 'We're going to make our way to church. Are you coming with us? It is Easter.'

Joe shook his head. 'I have an appointment with Feeney in less than an hour. I can't speak for Brenda.'

'I'm going with Joe,' Brenda said hastily. 'I don't want him to be on his own on the off-chance that someone else has a go at him.'

'Never one for church, were you Murray. Unless you were stealing the lead off the roof.'

'Console yourself, Les. The lead I allegedly nicked was sold for scrap, and probably melted down and then turned into bullets for you and your toy soldier friends.'

Les did not rise to the remark, and several minutes of idle chatter passed between the three women before Sheila, Sylvia and Les finally ambled off along the promenade, to the nearby church.

'Peter,' Brenda commented.

'Huh?' Joe had sunk into his thoughts once more, and Brenda's comment snapped him from them.

'Sheila. She goes to church at times like Easter and Christmas in memory of Peter.'

'I know. You don't bother?'

'Whatever spiritual side I had was knocked out of me when Colin died.' Brenda smiled wanly. 'And he didn't believe, you know.' She stood up. 'If we walk slowly, do you think it'll be ten o'clock by the time we get to the police station?'

'Probably not, but we can't sit here all day, can we?' Joe stubbed out his cigarette and they sauntered from the patio, out onto the pavement, and turned towards the town.

Not yet nine-thirty and already the seafront was busy with families and couples taking the fresh, spring morning air. Joe watched them with a sense of near-envy. He would not want their lives, but he would welcome their apparent peace.

'How come you've worked for me for five years and yet I know so little about you?'

Brenda guffawed causing a young couple to turn and stare.

'I think you know all of me, Joe.'

He laughed. 'That's not what I meant.'

'You're so wrapped up in the business, aren't you?' Brenda's laughter subsided. 'I mean, how much do you know about Sheila?'

'More than I do about you. I know Peter was a police inspector. I remember Colin from school and, naturally, I remember your wedding. I know he worked at the pit all his life, until it shut down, but I've no idea what he did after.'

There was a wistful element about Brenda's voice. 'He was the deputy manager when it closed, and he came into one hell of a redundancy payoff. Soon after that, the cancer was diagnosed. He carried on working as long as he could. Supervising in a warehouse. He was a good man, Joe, but he always felt we were cursed. No children, and then the cancer striking like that. He died too young.'

'That's a familiar tale in Sanford.'

They passed a public car park, its spaces filled with vehicles gleaming in the morning sunlight: some old, some new; saloons, people carriers, 4x4s, a brace of sports cars. Joe could visualise the owners. From rich to poor via moderately middle-class, the images rang through his head like a cross-section of society.

'Bank holiday, sunshine, nothing changes,' Joe muttered. 'Everyone makes for the seaside.'

'Wasn't it always like that? Even when we were kids, a day at the seaside was as important as the chocolate eggs.'

'Not for me. The café always came first. Even when Dad ran it.'

Passing the Winter Gardens and the pier, Brenda spoke again.

'You know, Joe, we all think of you as a successful small businessman, but I wouldn't have your life for twice the profits. Have you ever thought of jumping on a plane to Tenerife and seeing Alison?'

'You've had enough of me already?' he asked. 'That was quick… even by my standards.'

Brenda laughed again. 'That's not what I'm saying. I'm thinking of you, not me, and not us.'

At the corner of Regent Street and its busy, open, pedestrian area, he paused to roll a cigarette. When he had lit it, he walked on, following the promenade rather than heading into town.

'Yes, I've thought of it, but I don't see the point. I've told you before, the café came between us. That hasn't changed, and it's not likely to.'

With a sad shake of the head, Brenda said, 'I didn't mean with the object of getting together again. I meant just going to see her; as an old friend, not an ex-husband. The tropical sun would do you good and putting two thousand miles between you and the Lazy Luncheonette wouldn't do you any harm for a week or two. Maybe I'll talk to Sheila and we'll come with you.'

'After Wes Staines's wedding.'

Brenda screwed up her face. 'Huh?'

'Alec's boy. He's getting married in a couple of months. Remember? Alec has been nagging me to make it a STAC weekend so he can get us into the disco after the wedding. And he said you, Sheila and I would get invites to the wedding.' He snorted. 'As if I want to stand by watching some other poor sod sign his life away.'

'You're a cynical old bugger.'

'It's what comes of running a café in

Sanford.'

* * *

Chief Inspector Feeney was welcoming but had little more to tell them.

After supplying them with a cup of tea each, she said, 'We questioned the two attackers and they put us onto Freddie Delaney,' she reported. 'He found them in the bar and offered them fifty pounds to scare you off.'

'Cheap,' Joe commented.

Brenda grimaced at her beaker. 'Like the tea.' More brightly, she announced, 'Hazel Delaney tells us Freddie is innocent.'

'There are things about Freddie you don't know, Mrs Jump.'

'You mean like he's an ex-con?' Joe asked.

Feeney recoiled in surprise. 'You know?'

'I put it together from things Freddie said.' Joe grinned at her. 'I told you, I'm not as daft as I'm stupid looking. I guessed it and Hazel confirmed it last night.'

'Yes, well, in that case you'll know that he was in a similar position to Virginia Nicholson. We've had no problem with Freddie since he came to Weston, but it's obvious that Diane had her claws into him like she had with Ginny. Freddie, however, was a different prospect to Ginny. Tougher. If Hazel has confirmed it, you'll know that he was sentenced for an armed robbery in which a security man died. I don't know how Diane got onto him. Probably through Gil. He and

Freddie were on remand at Long Lartin together for a while. Anyway, when we learned Freddie had paid the two men to attack you, we went to the Leeward to see him, but he's gone. We have a nationwide hunt on for him, and when we catch up with him, he's going back to prison.'

'Whether he's guilty or not?' Brenda asked.

'We believe he is guilty, Mrs Jump, but it's irrelevant. Setting that pair on Joe is enough to send Freddie back to jail, and while he's there, we can carry on with our investigation.'

Brenda was about to protest again but Joe got there first. 'Ginny's murder doesn't make sense. Why would Freddie kill her?'

'I can't think of a single reason, Joe,' Feeney admitted, 'but then, I'm not saying Freddie killed her. I believe he killed Diane, and he used the same method as had been used on Ginny, probably in an attempt to mask his actions and divert attention from himself. We'll only know when we talk to him. For now, I know very little. It is Easter and I'm still waiting for the full forensic reports on both deaths.'

Joe turned a triumphant smile on Brenda, a smile that said, 'I told you so'. Turning his attention back to Feeney, he asked, 'Did you check Gil Shipton's and the Badgers' alibis at that pub?'

'The Castle Hotel? Yes. Sergeant Holmes was there yesterday afternoon while we were still questioning the others, and the landlord confirms that they were there all evening. It still doesn't mean it's true, of course, but with Freddie's disappearance we're confident that they had nothing to do with it.'

'Maybe we should call at the Castle and have a drink or two, Joe.'

Joe smiled at Feeney. 'What Brenda means is maybe she and I should go there and quiz the landlord.'

The chief inspector was not amused. 'Yes, I understood, but I don't like to see members of the public taking any risks, and you've already crossed Gil Shipton a couple of times. Naturally, I can't stop you, but…' She let the suggestion hang in the air.

Joe stood up. 'All right, Patricia. We'll get out from under your feet.'

Feeney, too, stood and showed them to the door. 'If you see anything of Freddie Delaney or you get any clue as to his whereabouts, don't be a hero, Joe. Call us.'

'You have my word on it.'

They stepped out into the mid-morning sunshine where Joe lit a cigarette.

'Any idea where this pub is?' Brenda asked.

'Haven't a clue.' He took out his street guide and studied it. 'Might help if we knew the address,' he muttered, and they walked away from the police station.

Ten minutes later, after learning it was on Clifftop Park Road, Joe and Brenda climbed into a taxi for the two-mile, five minute journey.

'What do we do when we get there?' Brenda asked as they drove past the Leeward and the driver turned right, inland, for the steep climb up to Clifftop Park.

'Ask him whether the Shiptons really were there on Friday night.' He smiled reassuringly at her. 'Just follow my lead, Brenda.'

When they arrived, they found both the pub and the beer garden packed, and the staff virtually run off their feet.

A large, rambling building, built of redbrick, it looked incongruous in the woodland around it, but there was no arguing its popularity. The sunshine, warm temperatures and the semi-rural location, adjacent to the park, ensured the bank holiday trade.

Inside, the open plan room was packed. Brenda found a table in front of which was a large crowd watching Sunday afternoon football on an overhead TV. Looking beyond the crowd, she could see Gil Shipton, Elaine and Terry Badger sat near the exit to the beer garden.

It took Joe the better part of ten minutes to get served, and it was a further five minutes before the landlord, James Burridge, finally appeared to talk to them.

In the meantime the presence of Gil and the Badgers did not escape Joe's attention, either. They appeared deep in conversation, but he had noticed Gil Shipton's eyes on him.

Burridge was a stout man in his late fifties, according to Joe's estimate. He sweated profusely in the rising heat of the busy bar, and his ruddy cheeks puffed out his breath as if demonstrating his stress levels. He stomped through the room towards them pausing at the bar only to snatch up the remote control for the TV and turned down the volume.

'I'm talking,' he snapped at the crowd when they complained, and switched his attention to Joe. 'And just who are you to be asking?' he demanded when Joe put the question.

'I'm a private investigator,' Joe half-lied, 'and Brenda, here, is my business partner.' He purposely injected some granite into his voice. 'I know guys like you. You'll tell the cops anything to keep them outta your hair. But since I'm not gonna be in your hair once I have my answers, you can tell me the truth.'

Burridge sat with them, and leaned on his elbows. 'So you want to know if Mr Shipton's party were here all night on Friday?'

Joe shook his head. 'Not all night, I just want to know whether they were here from, say, nine o'clock onwards.'

'And you already know I told the police they were?'

Joe felt his excitement rising. 'Yes. I do. I'm asking you for the truth, instead.'

'Right. I'll tell you the truth Mr private investigator.' Burridge glared. 'They came through those doors at half past eight.' He pointed to the main entrance. 'And they sat right where they are now, playing cards and talking until gone half past eleven, when I had to ask them to leave so I could lock up. As far as I know, they went up to their rooms.' With that, Burridge stood up and stomped away through the crowds surrounding the bar. Once again he snatched up the remote and this time turned the volume back up so the football watchers could hear the commentary.

Brenda swallowed half her glass of Campari. 'Well, that didn't work out too well, did it?'

'Suppose not,' Joe grumbled. He drank from his glass of lager. 'Proves my point though, doesn't it?'

Brenda eyed Burridge, now talking to Gil Shipton. 'What point?'

'If Gil, Elaine and Terry Badger were here all night, they can't have killed Diane, and who does that leave? It doesn't matter how much Hazel ignores it, the truth is Freddie did it.' He stared up at the TV. 'Although, when I come to think about it—'

'Right now, Joe, if we don't get out of here, there's likely to be another incident,' Brenda interrupted. 'And it'll concern me and you.' She finished her drink with one swallow and indicated Gil Shipton delivering a murderous glance in their direction.

Joe drained the rest of his ale, put the glass down, and stood up. 'I reckon you're right. Let's move.'

They stepped hurriedly out into the warm, spring air, and Joe put his mobile to his ear to call a taxi. A minute later, he said, 'It'll be five minutes.'

'Good. I think we're taking too many risks here, Joe, and…'

'Don't you ever learn, shorty?'

They turned to find Gil, Terry and Elaine behind them, and the sour look on Gil's face was impossible to misinterpret.

Joe swallowed hard. 'Listen, Shipton, I came here to prove you didn't kill your wife. I've just done that, so why don't you call it quits while you're ahead?'

'And what if I choose not to?' a malevolent smile crossed Gil's features. 'What if I feel the time's right to give you a good hiding.'

'You'd be making a big mistake,' Joe assured him. 'I'm not alone this time.' He gestured at Brenda.

Gil laughed. 'Then let's see how tough you both are, eh?'

He stormed forward, Brenda put herself in front of him and as he marched at her, determined to get to Joe, she kicked, landing her right foot between his legs.

The wind taken from him, in sudden agony, Gil fell to his knees.

'Get your mum to kiss it better,' Brenda snapped.

Terry and Elaine took a pace forward, but Joe stayed them. 'I wouldn't if I were you. I've seen Brenda put bigger than you down, Terry, and you won't want to get on the end of her handbag, Elaine. Now why don't we all just go our separate ways and hope our paths don't cross again?'

* * *

'The odds are on Freddie,' Joe said when they climbed out of the taxi outside the Leeward, 'but I spotted something in that pub and I need to test it out. I'm just gonna nip up to my room for a few minutes. I'll be back down in time for lunch.'

'Don't be late,' Brenda ordered. 'We have the Easter Bonnet Parade at three.'

'Five minutes,' he assured her as he passed through the bar and made for the lift.

He passed the time messing with the TV set in his room. Unlike the set in the pub, it was not modern. In fact, it took what seemed like an age to warm up, and when he checked the menu settings, he could not find what he was looking for.

Eventually, he gave up, and returned to the dining room where his fellows were already at their table tucking into roast beef and Yorkshire pudding. Ordering a glass of sweetened orange juice for starters, Joe ate ravenously, and as he did so, he gave Sheila an account of their unproductive morning. 'The only highlight was Brenda kicking Gil where he keeps his brains.'

'Well done, my dear,' Les Tanner applauded. 'Sounds to me like it's just what the fella needed.'

'That may be, Les, but the Shiptons of this world are not known for forgetting.' Sheila frowned. 'And now we have to worry about Brenda as well as Joe.' She focussed on Joe. 'So what you're saying is it looks more and more like Freddie?'

Joe nodded. 'I'm afraid so. Unless there's someone else involved, someone on the fringe who we don't know about. But then, we know for a fact that Freddie sicked those idiots onto me the other night and yesterday in Bath. It has to be him.' He glanced along the rows of tables to where Hazel was directing staff. 'It's that lass I feel sorry for.

She obviously loves him and she's praying he's innocent.'

Brenda sighed. 'And she's gonna be awfully let down.'

Chapter Twelve

Walking along the seafront towards the Winter Gardens, the four women carrying their Easter bonnets in opaque carrier bags as if they were closely guarded secrets, Alec Staines drew Joe's attention to the vehicles on the public car park.

'Time I was getting rid of my old van and getting something like that,' he said, with a wave at a maroon 4x4.

'Why would you need a gas guzzler like that, Alec?' Joe demanded. 'Most of your work is in Sanford.'

'Save me running two cars, Joe. I could get all my gear in that and then chuck it out of a weekend so I can take Julia out.'

Joe's eyes were distracted by a similar, silver grey vehicle parked at the rear of the car park. 'Take Julia for a bitta spring testing, you mean.' The Staineses were known for their bedroom antics, and in years gone by, Joe had dated Julia before Alec happened on the scene.

Where had he seen that car before?

'Jealous?' Alec said. 'Oh, listen, Joe, talking of testing the bed springs, you do know our Wes is getting married in the summer. I did ask if you'd put it to the membership as an official STAC outing. A few days in Windermere.'

Had he seen that car before?

Joe focussed on Alec. 'I haven't forgotten. There's a meeting next week. I'll put it to them then.'

'Well, if they won't go for it, I'll send invites for you and the harem.' Alec gestured at Sheila and Brenda walking alongside Julia ahead of them.

What was it about that car?

Joe snorted. 'Harem. Chance'd be a fine thing.'

'That's not what the rumour factory is saying, mate.'

'As long as they're talking about me and the girls, they're leaving everyone else alone.'

When they got to the Winter Gardens, it was to find Robert Quigley fussing over the arrangements, shepherding the women off to a side room where they could prepare for the parade.

Joe was slightly miffed to learn that everyone else, himself included, had to pay an admission fee of five pounds.

'I've already paid twenty pounds to enter the two women into the competition,' he protested.

'And good luck to them, Mr Murray,' Quigley said, 'but I'm afraid it will cost you another five pounds to watch them.'

'Are they coming out in bathing costumes?' Joe asked as he dug into his wallet.

'No. Easter bonnets.' Quigley smiled. 'It is for charity.'

Joe handed over the money. 'When I get home, I'm gonna found my own charity; The Joe Murray Poverty Appeal. Help old Joe back to solvency.'

There were one hundred entrants in the parade. And with an audience of about two hundred, Joe calculated that the charity appeal was cleaning up once more.

The competitors' role was simple. They literally paraded into the hall to the sound of Judy Garland singing *Easter Parade* alternating with the *Allegro* opening of Vivaldi's *Four Seasons*. As one piece of music finished, so the other started, and they repeated over and over, while four judges, one of whom was Quigley, sat in the background making notes. And when the contestants were all in the hall, they circled the area in front of the stage.

Joe and his STAC friends applauded vigorously when Sheila appeared with her floral design, Brenda with her farm animals, Sylvia with a small forest attached to her broad-brimmed hat. Julia had opted for a wedding theme, which to Joe's mind was another hint at their son's forthcoming wedding.

To his surprise, there were several men taking part, too. Most wearing gregarious headgear, with various designs; one had chosen a giant Easter egg planted on top of a trilby, while another had decked his oversized stovepipe hat with photographs of cars.

It was while staring at this ridiculous piece of millinery that realisation suddenly coursed through Joe… and with it came anger. 'The stupid, lying little cow,' he cursed.

Alec Staines was taken aback. 'Who? Brenda or Sheila.'

'No. I mean…' Joe trailed off at a furore coming from the back of the room.

At a signal from Quigley, the music stopped, the marchers ceased parading, and the organiser got to his feet.

To everyone's surprise, Elaine Badger pushed her way through the crowd and, facing Quigley, pointed at the stack of charity gifts on the left of the hall. 'I want the large egg my sister left there.'

'I'm sorry, er, miss, but those are charitable donations.'

'My sister donated it,' Elaine said. 'She's dead. That egg is now my property and I'm taking it back.'

'I'm afraid I can't—'

Elaine cut Quigley off. 'I'm not asking your permission. I'm taking it. Now.' She strode across to the stack.

Quigley's eyes travelled to the rear of the room. 'Get security in here, please.'

Joe stood. 'Leave her to it, Quigley. She's telling it like it is, and legally, I don't think you'd have much of a leg to stand on.' He stared sourly at Elaine. 'She's like her sister. Selfish and greedy. No, I take that back, she's worse than her sister. Greedier and more selfish. You're better off without contributions from her.'

Elaine snatched the egg from the stack, tucked it under her arm and strode back towards Joe. 'Loser.'

'I'd rather be a loser than a tart,' Joe retorted.

Gil appeared on the fringes of the crowd. 'Shoving your oar in again, shorty?'

Joe scowled at him. It was less the presence of other people, more his anger that gave him the courage to face up to Shipton. 'You're scum, pal, and one of these days, someone will do what they should do with you. Sweep you up and pour you down the drain.'

Elaine walked to Gil's side and he slipped an arm around her shoulder with a familiarity that surprised Joe. Gil grinned at Joe. 'If anyone's going to sweep me up, it won't be you, china.'

'No. I'll be in the audience applauding.'

Gil grinned. 'Only if you can get someone to lift you up so you can reach. See y'around, shortarse.'

'Not so fast.'

The voice of Chief Inspector Feeney stunned everyone. Gil and Elaine turned to face her and a squad of uniformed police.

With great formality, she intoned, 'Michael Shipton, Elaine Badger, I'm arresting you both for questioning on the murder of Terrence Badger.'

* * *

While Shipton and Elaine were taken away, the fuss in the hall died down, and Quigley made an effort to restore the parade, but met with little success. Interest had waned to the point where it was non-existent. A winner was declared, a local woman, who, with a shy, almost embarrassed smile, posed for photographs with her £20 voucher and wearing the bonnet, which reminded Joe of a small copse on top of a sheet of butcher's green.

'Well that explains why Diane was so miffed,' Brenda said, ignoring the presentation.

'Possibly,' Joe agreed, 'but it doesn't make any difference. They didn't kill her. Freddie did, and I know exactly where to find him.'

'You do?'

Joe nodded. 'Follow me.'

* * *

Five minutes later, Joe marched into the Leeward, asked Hazel to meet him in the bar, and then passed through the doors, nodded to Sheila and Brenda sat in the window dismantling their Easter bonnets, and strode to the bar, as Hazel arrived from reception.

'What can I get you, Joe?' she asked.

She appeared a little brighter than when he had first seen her at breakfast, but her eyes were still baggy and soulless.

'You can get me a good dose of the truth,' he replied, keeping his voice down.

Shock shot across her face. 'What?'

'I've just come out of the Winter Gardens where they've arrested Gil Shipton and Elaine Badger. Terry Badger has been murdered. Now, I can't say whether or not they killed him, but I can say your old man killed Diane, and I also know he's still here. Don't lie to me, Hazel. I've just seen his car on the car park down the road.' Joe pointed to the photograph behind the bar. 'Where is he?'

'Gone, I tell you. He didn't take his car—'

'Any man who loves his car enough to put a picture of it on the walls at his place of work, wouldn't go anywhere and leave it behind. Even if all he was gonna do was sell it, he'd take it with him. And why would he leave it on a public car park when you have a back yard where he normally parks it? He moved it and hid it amongst other cars on that car park, where plod were least likely to look, and then he walked back here. The old story of hiding a tree in a forest. Now stop taking the mick, and tell me where he is. Either that, or I bell Feeney and tell her to get out here.'

Hazel looked away, then back at him, then away again, this time with frustrated eyes. She brought her attention back to him, and pointed to the left. 'Take the lift to the third floor. I'll meet you there. There are two flights of steps to climb when you get there. You'll manage them, will you?'

'Do I look like I won't?'

Five minutes later, he was having second thoughts as Hazel ushered him from the top floor of residential rooms and up to the attics. The steps were steep and taxing, and by the time they arrived on the absolute top floor of the hotel, he was out of breath.

There were four small rooms at this level. Hazel rapped three times on the whitewashed door of one.

'Who is it?' her husband's voice came from within.

'Me. Hazel. Open the door.'

The sound of the lock snapping back reached Joe's ears. Freddie opened it, smiled at his wife, then spotted Joe. His smile turned to fury.

'What the bloody hell—'

'Knock it off, Freddie,' Hazel interrupted. 'He knows everything. At least he thinks he does.'

'You stupid, bloody woman. Do you know who he is?'

'She knows,' Joe butted in. 'She also knows I know you sent those goons after me the other night and in Bath yesterday.'

Freddie ignored him. 'His niece is a cop. He'll go straight to Feeney.'

Hazel opened her mouth, but Joe beat her to it again. 'Wrong. A couple of hours ago, I probably would have done, but things have changed and right now I don't know my arse from my elbow. Now let me in Freddie. You have to talk to me.'

There was a critical silence in which Freddie glared at Joe and his wife, and Hazel pleaded with her eyes. Eventually, he opened the door wide enough for his wife and Joe to enter. And as Joe came in, Freddie slammed the door shut and turned the key again.

It was a pitifully small room; smaller, Joe thought, than his flat over the Lazy Luncheonette. A tiny, dormer window looked to on the rear roof and yard of the hotel and the street beyond, a narrow back alley between the rear of the Leeward and a council car park mingling with the rear of other guest houses and hotels.

Inside the room, all Freddie had was a single divan bed, and a wooden chair on which stood his alarm clock, a half full ashtray and an empty plate and cutlery. He looked as tired as his wife; dishevelled, and he had not shaved – nor washed for all Joe knew.

'How are the mighty fallen?' Joe muttered.

Perching on the edge of the bed, his wife by him, holding his hand, Freddie screwed up his face into a question mark.

'There you were, lord of all you survey and now look at you. Hiding away in a dirty attic where I wouldn't hide my ex-wife.' Joe looked around for somewhere to sit, and there was nowhere but the chair. He cleared the clock and plate from it, put them on the bare floorboards and moved it back from the bed before sitting down. Anything to keep him beyond the range of those massive arms and large hands. Putting the ashtray on the floor beside the chair, he said, 'All right, Freddie. Start talking.'

'I've nothing to say.'

'Wrong. You've a lot to say. Like why did you send those guys after me on Friday night?'

'I didn't.'

'Nah, don't gimme that.' Joe shook his head. 'They told me to get back to Sanford. Now who in Weston-super-Mare knew I was from Sanford? Only you, your wife and the cops. I don't think Hazel did it, and I know the police didn't, and that means it could only be you. You sent 'em. Tell me why.'

Freddie tutted and scowled at his wife. 'Why is it if you want something doing, you're always better doing it yourself?'

Joe did not give Hazel time to answer. 'A question I constantly ask myself. Now why?'

The big man sighed. 'They were ordered not

to hurt you. I told 'em to scare you. Nothing more. I just wanted you to mind our own business.'

'Why? Because you'd been across to Diane Shipton's place and killed her? Or was there something about you that my inquiries might uncover?'

'There's a lot you don't know about me,' Freddie replied.

'True. But I know you're an ex-con, and you got half remission. It means you still have time to serve and being mixed up with a woman like Diane Shipton could be enough to send you back to finish your sentence.'

Freddie glowered at his wife. 'You told him, you silly cow? What is the point—'

Hazel backed off in horror. 'I had to. Jeez, Freddie, you don't know what he's like when he gets going. He's worse than the bloody beer salesmen. He won't let go.'

'She's right, Freddie.' Joe took out his tobacco. 'I never give in. And you know it, too. That's what I told you in the bar when I first mentioned Diane Shipton to you, and it's the reason you sent those clowns after me, isn't it? And, by the way, Hazel didn't tell me, she only confirmed it. You were the one who told me. You let it slip that you knew Diane, and that was enough for me to put it together. Now I've heard Hazel's line of logic on this business of you keeping your past a secret, but it doesn't make much sense. I'm not likely to go back to Sanford and start blabbing about how I stayed in a hotel run by an ex-armed robber, and even if I did, how much difference would it make to you in Weston-super-Mare? At the most you might lose a dozen customers over the next five years.'

Freddie eyed his wife. 'You were never the main worry.'

Spreading tobacco along a cigarette paper, Joe asked, 'Then who was? The filth?'

The big man looked at his wife, then back at Joe. 'I can't tell you.'

The gesture was not lost on Joe. 'You can't tell me, or won't tell me while your wife is here.'

Freddie did not answer and that confirmed Joe's suspicions. Freddie's shoulders slumped and he shook his head. 'I knew you were trouble, Joe. I bloody knew it.'

Joe grinned. 'Cut the compliments and let's hear it.'

'I have nothing to say. Get that. Nothing.'

Joe held up his completed cigarette and raised his eyebrows, asking permission to smoke it. Freddie nodded, and Joe lit the cigarette. Tucking his Zippo back into his pocket, he said, 'I believed Diane was putting the screws on you about your past, the way she did Ginny, and I believed you went out and murdered her for that very reason. The cops have just arrested Gil Shipton and Elaine Badger for Terry Badger's murder. That changed my thinking, because it doesn't make sense to me to have three different killers. So it changed my mind, but unless you let me help you, you'll go down for a murder I don't believe you committed. Now what is so bad that you can't help me to help you?'

Freddie shook his head. 'They've pulled in Shipton and Elaine Badger?'

'I was there when Feeney arrested them. Come on, pal. Talk to me.' The big man fumed, but remained silent. Joe drew on his cigarette. 'Honesty is what matters, mate. It won't get you anywhere doing a runner... or pretending to do a runner. At some stage the search for you will step up a gear. Someone else will see your car on that car park, and Feeney will come back, with a warrant next time. They'll go through this hotel like syrup of figs going through a baby. What will you do then? Hold one of the guests hostage?'

Frustration began to get the better of Freddie. 'Gar. It's all right for you to talk. You never wanted for nothing, did you? Brought up proper, you were. Privileged.'

Joe's anger spiked at the accusation. He crushed out his cigarette and replaced the ashtray on the floor. 'Privileged? Me? I'll tell you summat, shall I? From the age of ten, I was going to school, coming home then helping my old man in the café. Before I left school, I was crawling outta bed at half past five in the morning to give him a hand in the kitchen, and when I left school I went straight to work in the place. I had two days of college every week, and even then I had to get up at half past five to help him first. And I've done it all my life. Even now, I'm up at five every bloody morning, and I don't knock off until four in the afternoon, and after we've closed, I have the books to do, socks to heck and order. You think that's a privilege? Graft is what it is. Honest graft, and that's the difference between us, Freddie. Honesty. I pull the odd fast one, sure, but what businessman doesn't? But I don't look for the easy way out. I don't rob banks or security vans. I work for my living. Always have done.'

His rant over, Joe began to relax. Sat on the edge of the bed, Hazel holding his hand, her face a picture of concern, Freddie suddenly smiled.

'You've got a lot of bottle, Joe Murray, talking to an armed blagger like that.'

'What the hell is going down, Freddie?'

Freddie sucked in his breath and stood up. 'Do your civic duty, Joe. Call Feeney. Tell her where I am and I'll give myself up.'

Joe coughed in surprise. Hazel was stunned into anger. 'I've lied my head off for you over the last twenty-four hours and now you're gonna—'

'If they have Gil Shipton and Elaine Badger, it's time for me to go to the cops. Simple as that. And don't ask for any more cos I ain't giving you any.'

While Hazel appeared to be building up to shred her husband, Joe was more thoughtful. 'Tell me why you went to see Diane last night?'

Freddie thought about it. 'What does it matter? When I got there, I saw the cops, asked a few questions of the neighbours and when I found out what had happened, I knew I'd be fingered, so I legged it.' With a glance at his wife, Freddie went on. 'I had to go to her place. I couldn't talk to her anywhere else. Not with Gil and Terry around. I had to get her alone.'

Joe leapt to the obvious conclusion. 'And you

knew she'd be alone because I told you in the street that I'd faced them out in The Prince.' Freddie nodded. 'And you also asked Hazel to tell everyone that you were here all the time?' Joe asked and Freddie nodded again.

A glum silence fell over the tiny room. Joe tossed the information around his head, drawing various scenarios, not all of them pretty. 'You're still not telling me why you went to see her.'

'No. And I'm not going to. Now do like I said, and call Feeney. I ain't gonna put up a fuss.'

'What's so different now to earlier this morning?' Hazel demanded.

'He just told you,' Joe replied. 'They have Gil and Elaine.'

'And what difference does that make?'

Taking out his smartphone, Joe shrugged at her. 'You tell me.'

Chapter Thirteen

Feeney smiled sympathetically at Joe. 'I'm sorry, but Freddie refuses to say anything.'

Joe's frustration reached boiling point. 'He told me to ring you. Said he wouldn't make a fuss.'

'He was quite amicable at first, but the moment he learned we'd released Gil and Elaine, he clammed up.'

They were outside the police station enjoying a smoke, taking the balmy, early evening air, watching the sun as it dipped towards the western horizon. The moment Joe arrived, Feeney brought him up to date.

'We've had to release them. We have no evidence against them on any of the three killings. I'm sure we'll find some... somewhere... sometime, but for now, they're free.'

'And the fake egg?'

'Nothing. We scanned it, and it's empty.'

With the news that Gil and Elaine were free and Freddie had refused to talk, Joe's irritation grew. 'This is the most complicated investigation I've ever tackled, and it all hinges on Diane and Freddie. She must have spoken to him. Maybe after she tackled Ginny.' He blew out an angry stream of smoke. 'What the hell is it?'

'You've asked Hazel?'

Joe nodded. 'She knew nothing about Diane until this last couple of days.' He stubbed out his cigarette on a nearby waste bin and after ensuring the stub was cool enough, tossed it into the bin. 'Let me speak to him.'

'Joe, I don't know—'

'Are you married, Patricia?'

She shook her head. 'I was in a relationship. It went askew.'

'Then you know how much pressure wives or husbands can bring to bear. Since Hazel isn't here, I'll have to stand in for her.' Joe grinned. 'Let me speak to Freddie.'

Feeney capitulated, and there was a delay of about ten minutes while Freddie was brought to an interview room. Looking on through a CCTV monitor, Joe was annoyed to find him handcuffed.

'He has a history as an armed robber, Joe,' Feeney insisted. 'We take no chances with known, violent offenders.'

'He's not violent,' Joe argued. 'He may have been once over, but Hazel has cured that, I'm sure.'

'Nevertheless…' Feeney ushered him into the room.

Joe sat before Freddie and felt a wave of sympathy for the man. Three days back, his life had been perfect. Now it was in tatters.

'Freddie, I know you didn't kill Ginny, we're pretty certain you didn't kill Terry Badger. You're only suspected of killing Diane. Neither Chief Inspector Feeney nor I think you did that either. But you have to help me prove it. Why did Diane come to see you?'

He looked away and then back at Joe. 'No

deal.'

'She's dead, Freddie. So is Terry Badger. Whatever—'

'Gil is still alive and so is Elaine, and they're out on the streets. No deal.'

'If I find one piece of evidence against them, they're going down,' Feeney assured him. 'And I will find it eventually. Freddie, what is it? What are you hiding?'

'You think they can't damage me while I'm inside? You don't need any excuse to send me back to Long Lartin, Feeney. You can do it in the bat of an eyelid. For the last time, I'm saying nothing.'

His words rang around Joe's head, and merely raised more questions. Before he could work out the answers, his frustration got the better of him. 'And what about Hazel? You leave her to suffer, do you? People say my marriage fell to bits because I put my business before it. I won't have that. I did what I had to do, but there's more than a grain of truth in it. Some people insist that Alison was the best thing ever to happen to me, and they may be right. But I know I'm right when I say Hazel is the best thing that ever happened to you, and she's not scared of the future. Whatever you have to deal with, she's willing to tackle it with you. Now for God's sake grow up and tell us what the hell is going on.'

There was a long pause during which Freddie would not look at them. Joe fervently hoped Freddie was thinking it over, letting the message sink in.

But when he looked up, Freddie's face displayed no emotion other than anger. 'Go to hell... better yet, go somewhere a lot colder. You're the detective. You work out where.' He looked at Feeney. 'Is that it? Can we call it a day now and get me back inside where I belong?'

At a nod from the chief inspector, Freddie was escorted back to the cells. The moment he had left, Feeney shrugged at Joe. 'It looks as if you were wrong, Joe.'

Joe had his doubts. 'I don't think so. What did he mean by that? Go somewhere a lot colder? And what did he mean when he said you don't need an excuse to send him back to Long Lartin? You can only put him back for another seven and a half years?'

Feeney gave him a meaningful stare. 'I can't comment on that, Joe. Freddie could, but I can't. As for somewhere colder, did he mean Hell freezing over? I don't know. What I do know is, he has every reason to murder Diane, and I have to send him back to prison.'

Joe stood up, ready to leave. 'Don't be too hasty, Patricia. At least wait until tomorrow.'

'Must I keep reminding you that it's Easter? Nothing will happen until Tuesday at the earliest. Joe, you're clutching at straws. It's likely that Gil and Elaine were responsible for the deaths of Virginia Nicholson and Terry Badger. If so, I'm sure we'll get to them eventually. But they cannot have murdered Diane. We know exactly where they were when she was killed. As far as I'm concerned, unless I turn up evidence to the contrary, that leaves Freddie Delaney. He and Ginny were the only two people in this town who might have a motive for killing her.'

Joe shook his head. 'No. Gil and Elaine had a motive, too, as we saw in the Winter Gardens earlier. What's more, I have an idea how they could have done it while they were still at the Castle Hotel.'

* * *

By the time he got back to the Leeward, Joe felt thoroughly despondent. From his overnight position, convinced of Freddie's guilt, he had come full circle and was now convinced of his innocence, and the only stumbling block to demonstrating it was Freddie himself.

Once dinner was over, he met with Hazel in the bar.

'I'm sorry, luv, I tried every dirty trick in the book, including emotional blackmail, but he wouldn't say why Diane came here or why he went to see her the other night.'

Hazel's eyes were red and her cheeks baggy. Joe guessed she had not had much sleep.

'It's something bad. Something he must have kept from me.' She was pleading with Joe. 'What is it? I know about his record. He told me. It doesn't matter to me, so what can it be that's so bad he's keeping it from me?'

Sheila patted Hazel's hand. 'Try to keep calm, dear.' She turned to Joe. 'Perhaps if Hazel went to see Freddie, she could persuade him to tell the police.'

Joe shook his head. 'You know the rules, Sheila. He's being held for questioning and they won't allow him visitors. I struggled to persuade Feeney to let me see him.'

Brenda had been deep in thought. She snapped out of it and asked, 'Forgive me, Hazel, but have you thought that Freddie may have had some sort of relationship with Diane before he met you?'

Hazel sneered. 'And you reckon that would matter to me? You think I played the virgin between splitting up with my ex and settling down with Freddie? Besides, according to what he did tell me last night, sleeping with Diane Shipton would be like sleeping with fish fingers… while they were still in the freezer. Why do you think Gil Shipton is playing away from home?'

Joe's colour drained and in that moment, understanding dawned on him. 'That's it!'

They all looked to him.

'What?' Diane asked.

'What is it, Joe?' Sheila demanded.

Brenda laughed. 'He's decided he's putting fish fingers on the menu at the Lazy Luncheonette.'

'We already sell fish fingers for the kids," Joe snapped. "No, it's what Freddie said. Go to hell, or better yet, somewhere colder. For crying out loud, it's been staring me in the face since Friday morning. Hazel. Quick. I need your help.'

* * *

The sun had dipped towards the horizon when Joe's taxi pulled up outside the rooming house on Clevedon Street.

To Joe, the place looked like any other seaside boarding house. Three storeys high, its brick stone front facing out across the town to the sea, the stone lintels of its windows were painted in brilliant white, expressing the cleanliness of coastal living. But the paint on the front door was fading, badly in need of another coat, and the fading sunlight on the windows reflected the dust. They hadn't been cleaned in a long time.

As he climbed out of the taxi, holding a large carrier bag, Chief Inspector Feeney and Sergeant Holmes got out of their unmarked car, and a gaggle of uniformed officers, male and female, climbed out of other cars.

'You're sure of yourself, Joe?' Feeney asked.

'Absolutely. Freddie is innocent and I know why he wouldn't speak.' The chief inspector invited further comment with a brief flicker of the eyebrows. 'He's a lifer, isn't he? That's what he meant when he said you could send him back to Long Lartin, and that's what you meant when you said you couldn't comment. Isn't it?'

Feeney nodded slowly.

'Hazel doesn't know, either,' Joe said. 'He told her he was the wheelman in that robbery, but he wasn't, was he?'

Feeney sighed. 'You're a clever man, Joe Murray.'

'And that's what this is all about,' Joe said. 'He lied to Hazel and he doesn't want her finding out the truth. Safer to go to prison for a crime he didn't commit, and then wait for you to turn up evidence against Gil and Elaine, then he would be released again, with Hazel never any the wiser.'

'And what difference does it make if Gil and Elaine are free?' Feeney asked.

'They have the same information as Diane. They could bring it out, or use it to shut him up.' Joe glanced up at the house. 'For now we'd better get Gil and Elaine before they scarper. You might struggle to prove it, mind. With their track record, I don't think they'll admit everything so freely.'

Feeney eyed the carrier bag. 'What's that for?'

Joe laughed. 'A present for the happy couple.' He nodded towards the house. 'Are they still here?'

Feeney, in turn, nodded to a dark BMW parked across the street. 'Gil's car.'

Joe grunted. 'I'll let you lead the way.'

The chief inspector detailed Holmes and two uniformed officers to approach the door where they rang the bell. On the first floor, the net curtain parted a little, then fell shut.

'Do it,' Feeney instructed.

A uniformed officer took a ram to the door three times before it smashed open. They hurried in. Feeney and Joe followed at a more leisurely pace to find Gil Shipton and Elaine Badger pinned on the stairs by police officers.

'What the hell is going on, Feeney?' Gil demanded.

'I have a warrant to search Flat three, Mr Shipton, for evidence pertaining to the deaths of

Virginia Nicholson, Diane Shipton, and Terrence Badger. If you obstruct my officers from carrying out that search, you will be arrested and charged. Sergeant Holmes?'

Holmes guided the couple back up the stairs, Feeney followed and Joe fell in behind her. Pushing into the flat, they found the place a mess. Clothing, books, magazines, Diane's personal effects were spread all over room.

'Someone ransacked the place,' Elaine said. 'We were trying to tidy up.'

'Then why did you just try to run?' Joe asked.

Gil scowled malevolence. 'Don't you think we've had enough hassle off the filth… and you?'

Careful to keep himself out of range of Gil's ham-like fists, Joe looked at the TV set, and grinned to himself. 'Score another point for Joe Murray,' he muttered.

He stepped around a heap of clothing and picked up the remnants of a giant Easter egg box. It was surrounded by a mass of torn gold foil, and beneath it, neatly cleaved in two were the halves of a plastic display egg.

He picked up the empty halves of grey plastic, badly sawn in half, and showed them to Feeney. Smiling at Gil, he said, 'You're lying. You were looking for something. But Chief Inspector Feeney told me it wasn't in this egg. They checked it at the police station with one of those airport type scanners. And I'll tell you something else. I knew it wasn't in this egg, because when I picked it up at the Winter Gardens, the foil wrapping hadn't been disturbed. If Diane had opened that and hidden it in here, no way could she have wrapped it up that expertly. And that's why you're tearing the place apart. You didn't find it in the fake egg, so you were still looking.'

'Where is it, Shipton?' Feeney demanded.

'Where's what?'

'You know damn well what. The information Diane threatened you with.'

'I don't know what you're talking about. We ain't got nothing, have we, Elaine?'

She shook her head. 'Nothing. I told you—'

'They're telling the truth, Chief Inspector,' Joe interrupted. 'They didn't find it.' He grinned at Elaine. 'Did you?'

Elaine brazened it out. 'I don't know what you're talking about.'

'You know your big mistake, don't you?' Joe asked. 'You were too quick to take that fake egg back from the charity stack in the Winter Gardens. If you'd waited and had a quiet word with Quigley later on, you might have got away with it. But no, you had to rush in, didn't you? Eager to get your mitts on it before the cops did. Keen to show everyone how hard-faced you can be.'

With more than a hint of frustration in her voice, Feeney asked, 'What is going on, Joe?'

'It's all quite simple, and some of it is down to my good friends Sheila Riley and Brenda Jump. Sheila's late husband was a police inspector. She knows how the law operates. She's intelligent and logical. When I come up with a theory, you can bet Sheila throws up the objections, and this time was no exception. When I thought Freddie Delaney had killed Diane, it was Sheila who asked where the argument between Gil and Diane came into it. I thought I had the answer. I thought Freddie was working for them. Especially after you told me he served time with Gil. But when we were all in the Winter Gardens this afternoon, watching Elaine's performance, it was Brenda who pointed out what everyone else had missed.' Joe stared at Gil and Elaine. 'The other woman in the Shipton's infernal triangle was Elaine. She and Gil were having an affair, and that's why Diane was so set against it. She didn't want Gil. He could please himself who he went with; but not her sister. So she logged all the details of their past crimes and stored it on a memory stick, which she then hid from them. The proposition was simple. Gil stops his carryings on with Elaine, or Diane handed everything over to the cops. She was willing to claim that Gil forced her to blackmail their victims. That way she'd get off with probation or at worst a light sentence.'

'We'd already guessed most of this,' Feeney objected.

'Yes, I know you had, but you couldn't prove it. I can. Y'see, there was something odd about it all, something I heard Diane say to Gil in that pub. He would never be able to find the information once the charity stock went off to the orphanages. But she would. Now how could she do that? She had no more idea than anyone where the giant Easter egg would end up. Some of my people suggested she had a tracking device on it. Nonsense. You can have parcels tracked, but for an individual to pay to have something tracked, is incredibly expensive and it demands knowledge of technology these people simply didn't have. No. Diane knew she'd be able to find it because she never put the memory stick in the charity egg in the first place.'

Joe let the two halves of the plastic egg drop and picked up his carrier bag. Digging into it, he came out with another giant Easter egg, which looked exactly the same as the fake one. He held it up so Elaine's greedy eyes could fall upon it. Without warning, he tossed it to her.

'Here. Try this one.'

'Joe, no. She'll crush it underfoot—' Joe cut Feeney off with a finger to his lips.

They watched as Elaine tore feverishly at the carton, then the wrapping, and finally emerged with a large chocolate egg. She broke it. Pieces of chocolate fell everywhere, and amongst them was a small packet of sweets.

Falling to her knees, searching feverishly through the detritus, tearing open the cellophane wrapping of the sweets, she eventually stood up. 'Nothing there.'

Joe smiled. 'I know.' He fished into the top pocket of his gilet and brought out a memory stick. 'I found it about half an hour ago.' He gestured at the mess on the floor. 'That's not the egg Diane left behind. It's a replacement which I bought on my way over here.'

Elaine's face turned to a mask of fury. She launched herself at Joe. A policewoman grabbed and restrained her. Gil moved, but Sergeant Holmes and Constable Tetlow restrained him.

Joe handed the memory stick to Feeney.

'Go on,' the chief inspector invited.

'When Diane came to Weston, it wasn't to blackmail Ginny or Freddie, it was to ask a favour. Ginny wouldn't listen. She'd already suffered at their hands years ago. So Diane made her way to the Leeward and asked Freddie. He listened. All she wanted was for him to keep the Easter egg safe, and he obliged, by putting it in his freezer... a place colder than Hell.' Joe laughed. 'And she had unwrapped and re-wrapped that egg. It wasn't perfect, but it would pass a casual inspection. Diane was smart. If and when Gil and Elaine stopped seeing each other, she could go back and collect it. And if Gil didn't toe the line, she could still go back and collect it but hand it over to you. She knew they were watching her every move, so she picked up the fake Easter egg, and put it out in full, public view. Unfortunately, it backfired on her. Convinced that they knew where the information was, there was only one way Gil and Elaine could get it back. They had to kill Diane so that it became the rightful property of her heir... Gil.'

Shipton spat at the floor. 'Prove it.'

Joe grinned. 'I don't have to. I'm sure the police will turn up the necessary evidence in good time, and they'll know exactly where to find you, Gil... in the nick, for a long time, I should imagine, once they get to Diane's information.'

Chapter Fourteen

Through the windows of the flat, Feeney and Joe watched Elaine and Gil taken away in separate cars.

'What about Ginny and Terry Badger?' the chief inspector asked.

Joe shrugged. 'You'll have a hard time proving all this, but my guess is they hit Ginny because she wouldn't tell them where the memory stick was hidden. She couldn't because she didn't know. I saw her and Freddie talking seriously at the bar in the Leeward on Thursday night. She was telling him about the incident with Diane. Freddie wasn't as worried as he made out because Diane had already been to see him, but when Ginny was murdered on Friday morning, he got nervy. In a straight fight, he might beat Gil or Terry, but he couldn't take them both together, and he was worried that he might be next. The fact is, they obviously didn't know Diane had visited Freddie, too, otherwise he really would have been next.'

'They couldn't have killed Diane, Joe,' Feeney pointed out. 'Remember the TV? Someone had to be here to turn up the volume while they murdered Diane, and we know for a fact that all three were in the Castle Hotel at the time.'

Joe tutted. 'What is it with you people and technology?' He began to search the mess on the floor. 'My friend Brenda took part in that TV programme; *I-Spy*. I bought one of these flatscreen

TVs for the café so my customers could watch her making a fool of herself. I don't watch telly, but I do like fiddling with... ah. Here it is.' He bent and picked up the remote for the TV. Aiming it at the set, he switched on and the volume almost blew their eardrums. Joe turned it down. 'I have to admit that it only occurred to me when I was in the Castle Hotel today, and I saw the landlord faffing with the telly. When I tried it with the portable TV in my room at the Leeward, it didn't work because it's an old set.' He waved at the TV. 'This is modern. Like the one I have in the café, only smaller. Now, watch this.' Reading the remote, he cautiously picked the right buttons. 'When they go on holiday, most people set up security timers for their lights. Modern TV sets have timers inbuilt, so you can arrange for the TV to come on while you're away, too, and any wannabe burglar will think you're home.'

A small menu appeared on screen, allowing the user to set up the on and off times. On the 'on' section of the menu, the time was set at 21:15.

'It's programmed to come on at nine fifteen, and look at the volume setting.' Joe gestured at the screen where the volume was set to seventy-five. 'Most of us don't need it higher than about ten or eleven,' he said. 'They killed Diane earlier, knowing that you would question them, and they used the TV to set up an alibi. Pathologists are always hazy about the time of death. When I checked with the landlord of the Castle Hotel, he assured me they were all there from half past eight onwards, and they never left the bar until about eleven. Everyone here heard the TV come on at a quarter past nine, and it led you to the assumption that Diane had been murdered then, but in fact, she was probably killed an hour earlier.'

'Clever,' Feeney congratulated him. 'And Terry?'

'You haven't told me anything about his death, so again, I can only speculate, and you're just as good at that as me. He was a bit of a dork, wasn't he?'

'Not the brightest star in the night sky, no. And, by the way, he was bludgeoned, the same as the others. With the same weapon by the looks of it.'

'I wonder if he knew about Gil and Elaine. If he didn't and then suddenly found out, last night, say, there would have been an argument and either Gil or Elaine finished it with the heavy duty spanner.' Joe shrugged. 'Like I said, you'll have a hard time proving it all.'

Feeney tossed the memory stick in the air, caught it, smiled and kissed it. Joe recognised the gesture as a surrogate kiss for himself. 'There's no rush. Not while we have them locked away for whatever is on this thing. And if we find one trace of either of them on the bodies, we'll have them.' She beamed a broad smile at him. 'Why didn't Freddie come to us with the Easter egg? If he'd brought it to us, we'd have arrested them earlier.'

'I'm guessing here, Patricia, but you have to understand that Freddie had no way of knowing what was in that egg. Diane probably told him it was important to her, but she wouldn't have said why. What if he brought it to you and there was nothing in it but chocolate? That would have alerted Gil and Elaine to the fact that Diane had been to the Leeward, and they would have targeted him. Even when he hinted to me where I could find it, he had no way of knowing whether it would save his skin.'

'Well, anyway, we have them now, and the evidence on that memory stick is enough for us to remand them in custody, which gives us plenty of time to pin the murders on them. And it's all thanks to you, Joe.'

He smiled modestly. 'Don't let Sheila or Brenda hear you say that.'

Feeney's placid features darkened. 'There is the matter of Freddie, though. I still can't work out what he was playing at.'

'It's called love, Patricia. I'm no good at it. I tried and failed. Freddie loves Hazel and she loves him. But when he came to Weston, he told her he got a fifteen-year sentence and he had nothing to do with the weapons used in the robbery. He didn't even let her in on that until he had a secure job and his feet under the table. Tell me what really happened on that robbery.'

Feeney nodded. 'Freddie shot the security guard. He pleaded manslaughter, but the jury wouldn't have it. It was murder during the course of an armed robbery. And he didn't serve seven and a half years as he told Hazel. He was given life, and he served fifteen before he was released on licence.'

'And you can send him back for a bar fight if

you want, can't you?' Joe waited for her to nod. 'He never told Hazel because he didn't want to scare her off. Over the years, he's been comfortable in that lie. After all, what was the danger? No one in Weston knew him, and the chances of someone from Long Lartin turning up here were pretty remote. Then Diane showed up, and she did know. If you check up, you'll maybe find that she covered the story when she was a reporter. Read through the information on that memory stick, and you'll find that she blackmailed him, too. By now, he couldn't afford to let Hazel find out. He was afraid he'd break her heart, maybe push her into tearing up their marriage lines. So he did as Diane asked. Then I started shoving my nose in and he knew I had a reputation for getting to the bottom to things. I told him that, my girls told him, too. He knew you couldn't say anything to me, and all he had to do was scare me off. Hence the two goons he sent after me.'

'I'm astonished that you got all that.'

Joe grinned diffidently. 'To be honest, I checked the memory stick before I brought it here, and it confirmed the background. The rest is intelligent guesswork.' He held up his hands. 'I had to. You wouldn't want me turning up with a porno movie starring Elaine and Gil, would you?'

Feeney laughed. 'No. I suppose not.' Her face became more serious. 'Freddie is a lifer, Joe. I could send him back for those two who attacked you.'

'You'd need a formal complaint.'

'You've already made one.'

'Then I withdraw it.' Joe shook his head. 'He was trying to protect himself and his wife, and what they'd built up over the last few years, and I'm not gonna send him back to the nick for that. I'm not sure I wouldn't have done the same in his position. And anyway, it was Hazel who tipped you off when they followed me to Bath.'

'I can't let it pass that easily, Joe. One of the things they teach you in the police is never let anything pass. If you see a car parked on double yellow lines, you don't ignore it because if you do, the driver will assume he has the right to park on double yellows lines. Freddie used intimidation. If I don't take some action, he may assume he can get away with it every time.'

'Push those two thugs. I don't think they followed me to Bath off their own bat. I think Gil Shipton learned that Freddie had paid them, and he paid them more to follow me and do a better job.' Joe smiled at her frown. 'Come on. You don't have to live your life by the book. If you feel the need to say something to Freddie, make it off the record. There was no harm done.'

There was a long pause before Feeney nodded. 'I'll see what I can do.'

* * *

The bar was crowded for the last night. While the DJ set up his equipment and allowed a Beatles album to run through its tracks, Joe, Sheila and Brenda sat by the windows reflecting on the last four days, and the prospect of getting back to normal after the long journey back to Sanford.

'I said before, I'm looking forward to it,' Joe told them.

'Looking forward to getting back into profit, you mean,' Brenda said.

Sheila backed her up. 'And while you're taking all that money, you'll be telling the draymen what a hero you were in Weston. How you saved the innocent man from the clutches of the police, and helped put the guilty away.'

Feeney had called before dinner and brought Freddie back to the hotel.

Sitting outside, she explained, 'I did like you said and gave him a verbal warning. It should be enough. By the way, you were right about those two. Freddie paid them fifty pounds initially. We don't know how Gil learned of it. They were probably talking their drunken heads off and he overheard, so he offered them a hundred each to follow you to Bath and do the job properly. But one condition was they had to ring Freddie and tell him. Our guess is that Gil was trying to deal with you and incriminate Freddie even further.'

Joe nodded. 'I think Freddie is a good guy at heart.' Lighting a cigarette, he asked, 'So did you check the memory stick?'

'Just as we suspected.' Feeney narrowed her eyes on him. 'Just as you already knew. It's a detailed history of their blackmail. The victims, the information they had on those people, the amounts... right down to the level of intimidation employed by Gil and Terry. Even if we don't get them for the murders, both Gil and Elaine are going down for a long time.'

'But they're not admitting anything? With regard to the murders, I mean.'

Feeney, too, lit a cigarette and blew a fine stream of smoke into the evening air. 'They're hardened, career criminals, Joe. They know the value of keeping their mouths shut. We're going to need testimony from the victims. A part of the deal I came to with Freddie was a full statement on what Diane had done to him in the past. She took him for five thousand pounds, you know. We'll need more than that, of course, but it's a start. If we can persuade one or two more victims to speak out, we'll have them.'

'And the murders?' Joe asked.

Feeney took another drag on her cigarette and shook her head. 'Different proposition. They've both denied everything, so it's down to forensics.' Abruptly she changed the subject. 'I hope this hasn't put you off Weston-super-Mare.'

He laughed. 'It should do, but no, it hasn't. Actually, I find it a pleasant little place. Maybe I'll think about retiring here.'

She chuckled. 'A Yorkshireman leaving his precious homeland? It doesn't sound likely.' Feeney stood and shook hands. 'Thanks, Joe. For everything.'

She left and soon after, Joe had joined his friends in the bar for the last night disco. It was an event which Joe often ran, but here, as in other hotels where they had stayed, the management preferred to get their own people.

And it was while waiting for the DJ to begin

that Freddie and Hazel both left the bar and, carrying a bottle of champagne, joined the trio by the windows.

'A little thank you, Joe,' Freddie said, placing the bottle and three glasses on the table.

'Oh goody,' said Brenda. 'I love bubbly.'

'You didn't have to,' Joe protested, but the Delaneys overrode his protest and poured for them.

'You'll join us?' Sheila invited.

Hazel shook her head. 'Busy night, we can't afford to get drunk yet. Maybe later, if you fancy a nightcap.'

They nevertheless sat down.

'You two are okay now, are you?' Joe asked.

Hazel nodded. 'Freddie has told me everything. The truth this time. And I've told him he's sleeping in the attic for the next three months for lying to me.' She winked to show she was only joking.

Joe laughed. 'Serves you right, too.' More seriously, he went on, 'You know, Freddie, I'm a total stranger to the kind of life you've led, but I've had people try to blackmail me in the past.'

'His ex-wife,' Brenda teased. 'She threatened to tell the absolute truth about him unless he bought her a diamond ring.'

'Ignore her,' Joe advised. 'One glass of champagne and she's anybody's.'

'I haven't touched the shampoo yet,' Brenda protested.

'All right, so one glass of Campari and she's anybody's.' Joe smiled at Brenda. 'I was saying,

I've had people try to intimidate me, too. I haven't suffered the way you did, but I've had them threaten to call Environmental Health if I didn't hand over a hundred. Know how I got round it?'

Freddie grinned. 'No, but I bet you're gonna tell me.'

'Yep. And it's easy. You just be up front about everything. I don't know what happened all those years ago, but I do know you're not the same man now as you were then.' Joe smiled at Hazel. 'Your missus persuaded me of that. Tell me something. What did you expect to gain by keeping your mouth shut?'

'The way I had it figured, Feeney would have nicked Gil and Elaine eventually, I'd have appealed, they would have let me out again. And Hazel would never have been any the wiser.'

'Just as I told Feeney,' Joe commented with a glow of pride.

Sheila wagged a finger at Freddie. 'No secrets. Not between a man and his wife.'

'I know about it all, now,' Hazel said. 'And I forgive him.' She hung onto her husband's arm.

'You should be honest with others about it, too,' Joe said. 'If the people of this town knew about you, it might make them wary, but it would also make them study you, and once they knew you were to be trusted, they'd come round. And when everybody knows about you, no blackmailer can ever have a hold over you.'

A deafening blast from the speakers heralded the opening bars of Abba's *Dancing Queen*, calling Sheila and Brenda to the dance floor, and drowning out Freddie's response.

'Say again,' Joe shouted.

Freddie frowned in the direction of the DJ, then leaned closer to Joe. 'I said, you make sense, but I'll have to give it some thought. When me and a few others hit that security van, I was a young kid. I needed the money and I wasn't too fussy where or how I got it. None of us meant for the security bloke to die, but he did, and I have to live with that and the shadow of the nick hanging over me for the rest of my life. That's hard enough, Joe. Whether I can ride out the wagging tongues on the back of it, I don't know.'

'Think about it.' Joe smiled at Hazel. 'There's a lady who'll stand by you.' Putting down his glass, he asked, 'Why did you go to see Diane last night?'

'To ask her to take that bloody Easter egg back,' Freddie replied. 'I got jittery after Ginny was killed, and then when Feeney arrested those two idiots in Bath, I got really nervous, so I took the egg with me.' He smiled wanly. 'Course, when I got there and saw the place crawling with cops, and I found out what had happened, I panicked. I thought I'd better disappear, quick.'

'I can understand that,' Joe said. 'That doesn't make it sensible or right, but I can understand it. Did you know what was in the egg?'

Freddie shook his head. 'Didn't have a clue. I thought it might contain incriminating evidence, sure, but I didn't know. Then I heard you prattling about how she'd put the other egg on the charity stand in the Winter Gardens, and I figured she was playing some kinda bluff, but I didn't know which egg was which, so I was going to insist she take it back. As long as we had it, we were in danger... well, Hazel was.'

'Why didn't you just hand it over?' Joe asked. 'Even when the law came to pick you up, you still kept quiet.'

'I wasn't thinking straight, Joe,' Freddie confessed. 'First off, like I say, I didn't know which egg was which. What if I'd given it to Feeney and there was nothing in it? It could have made things worse for me. Then, I figured with Diane dead, it was insurance of a kind. As long as I had it, I could hold Gil at arm's length. I mean, if I didn't know what was in it, neither did he, and if there was nothing in it, he wouldn't ever have bothered me anyway.'

'Yet you gave me a hint. What changed your mind?' Joe asked.

'You did. You pointed out that Hazel was the best thing ever to happen to me, and she was ready to face the future. So I took the chance that you'd find it and know how to use it.' Freddie's beamed his broad smile again. 'Twenty years back, I'd have ripped Gil Shipton and Terry Badger apart, Joe, and it would never have been an issue. These days...' He patted his belly. 'Let's just say, I ain't the man I was.'

Joe smiled and eyed Brenda and Sheila dancing with George Robson. 'That goes for most of us, mate. You two look after yourselves.'

Freddie wandered off, couples took to the dance floor and with the end of *Dancing Queen*, the women returned to the table and Brenda took a healthy hit of champagne.

'You don't half tell some tall stories, Joe.'

'I don't know what you mean.'

Sheila disapproved with a cheeky smile. 'Blackmail? You've never been blackmailed in your life.'

'Yes I have. That bloke—'

'He was from Environmental Health,' Sheila interrupted, 'and he didn't ask for a hundred pounds. He warned you if you didn't clean up your act, you'd be *fined* a hundred pounds.'

'It amounts to the same thing in my book. Demanding money with menaces.'

Chapter Fifteen

With a gaping yawn, Joe unlocked the door to let in Sheila and Brenda.

'Morning, boss,' Sheila greeted.

'Shut your mouth, there's a bus coming,' Brenda said.

Joe closed the door and returned to table five, to read the morning newspaper.

It was seven o'clock on Tuesday morning, and the Lazy Luncheonette was open for business after the Easter break. But so far, there had been no customers.

Joe had spent much of the six-hour journey back to Sanford the previous day alternately sleeping and running the laptop on battery to bring his notes up to date.

He joined his friends at the Miner's Arms for a few drinks, and Alec Staines had pestered him again regarding his son's forthcoming wedding. Joe had promised to put the proposition to the membership at the earliest opportunity. At ten o'clock, almost exhausted, he had walked home, and by eleven, he was in bed sound asleep.

The alarm terrorised him at five in the morning and he dragged his weary bones into the shower, before coming down to the café and letting Lee in at six.

Banging and clanging about in the kitchen, Lee was his usual sunny self, and when they arrived, it seemed to Joe that Sheila and Brenda were just as tired as he, yet they maintained their air of indefatigable good cheer. He often wondered how they did it. The Lazy Luncheonette was his business, and it was successful, but it did little to cheer him up.

Once changed into their tabards, the two women began to busy themselves around the café, putting out sauces and condiments. Joe folded away his newspaper, disappeared into the back for a moment and came out with the float for the till.

Opening the drawer, he began dropping coppers and silver into the compartments, and under the clip for the notes, he found a receipt.

Studying it, he called out, 'Lee, what's this receipt in the till?'

His giant nephew appeared at the kitchen door his chef's hat cocked at a jaunty angle. He looked at the receipt and passed it back to Joe. 'It's for Danny's Easter egg. Remember, you told me to take some money out of the till and buy him one cos you'd forgot.'

Joe studied the faded print. His features paled, his face took on its usual mask of irritation. 'Fifteen quid? You spent a fifteen notes on a bloody chocolate egg?'

'Well you never said how much, Uncle Joe, so I just went into Mr Patel's next door and bought the biggest egg I could find.'

'Fifteen quid on a chocolate, bloody egg? You half-wit. You brainless, stupid, gormless...'

Across the café, Sheila watched the argument develop. 'Nice to be home, isn't it, Brenda?'

Brenda, too, watched their friend and boss

berating his nephew. 'Yep. Everything back to normal.'

THE END

THANK YOU FOR READING. I HOPE YOU HAVE ENJOYED THIS BOOK. WOULD YOU BE KIND ENOUGH TO LEAVE A RATING OR REVIEW ON AMAZON?

The Author

David W Robinson retired from the rat race after the other rats objected to his participation, and he now lives with his long-suffering wife in sight of the Pennine Moors outside Manchester.

Best known as the creator of the light-hearted and ever-popular **Sanford 3rd Age Club Mysteries**, **Mrs Capper's Casebooks** and in a similar vein the Spookies Paranormal Mysteries. He also produces darker, more psychological crime thrillers as in the **Feyer & Drake** thrillers and occasional standalone titles sometimes under the pen name **Robert Devine**

He, produces his own videos, and can frequently be heard grumbling against the world on Facebook at https://www.facebook.com/dwrobinsonauthor and has a YouTube channel at https://www.youtube.com/user/Dwrob96/videos. For more information you can track him down at www.dwrob.com and if you want to sign up to my newsletter and pick up a #FREE book or two, you can find all the details at https://dwrob.com/readers-club/

By the same Author

The Sanford 3rd Age Club Mysteries

A decade on from their debut, there are 26 volumes and a special in the Sanford 3rd Age Club Mystery series.

We follow the travels and trials of amateur sleuth Joe Murray and his two best friends, Sheila Riley and Brenda Jump. The short, irascible Joe, proprietor of The Lazy Luncheonette in Sanford, West Yorkshire, jollied along by the bubbly Brenda and Sheila, but only his friends, but also his employees, all three leading lights in the Sanford 3rd Age Club (STAC for short). And it seems that wherever they go on their outings on holidays in the company of the born-again teenagers of the 3rd Age Club, they bump into… MURDER.

A major series of whodunits marinated in Yorkshire humour, they are exclusive to Amazon and free to read for subscribers to Kindle Unlimited. The publisher, Darkstroke Books will close later this year and the publishing rights are reverting in blocks of five. You can find the newer editions at: https://mybook.to/stacser and if you wish to read those still attributed to Darkstroke Books, you can find them at: https://mybook.to/stacser

Mrs Capper's Casebooks

Christine Capper is a solid, down to earth Yorkshire lass, witty, plain spoken, but with an innate sense of inquiry (all right, then, she's nosy). She passes her days in the West Yorkshire town of Haxford looking after her long-suffering husband, Dennis, a man with an obsession for all things automotive, and putting him right when he goes wrong, which is more often than not. She takes care of their pet, Cappy the Cat, a feline with attitude, dotes on her granddaughter Bethany, and is openly proud of her son, Simon, now Acting Detective Constable Capper of the Haxford force.

A former police officer, she's Haxford's only trained and licenced private investigator. She's choosy about the cases she takes on but appears destined to be dragged into more serious affairs, during which she passes on her findings to her friend, Detective Sergeant Mandy Hiscoe and Mandy's immediate boss, DI Paddy Quinn, a man who is quite open about his dislike for private eyes.

A series of light-hearted mysteries, laced with Yorkshire grit and wit, Mrs Capper's Casebooks are exclusive to Amazon available for the Kindle and in paperback.

You can find them at:
https://mybook.to/cappseries

The Spookies Paranormal Mysteries

The misadventures of Lady Concepta (aka Sceptre)Rand-Epping and her two ghost-hunting partners, private eye Pete Brennan and ducker and diver, Kevin Keeley, not forgetting Sceptre's ghostly butler, Fishwick as they tackle bad guys from this world and the Other Side.

A series of light-hearted ghost hunts mingled with more earthly crimes. Learn more at:
https://dwrob.com/spookies/

Other Works

I also turn out darker works such as The Anagramist and The Frame with Chief Inspector Samantha Feyer and civilian consultant Wesley Drake.

For details visit https://dwrob.com/the-dark/

Printed in Great Britain
by Amazon